A FINAL REST

BLYTHE BAKER

～

A deadly welcome...

On her return to London, Rose Beckingham's reunion with her relatives is marred by shadows from the past. When a family wedding moves the party to the English countryside, it isn't long before old resentments resurface and dark suspicions are awakened.

With a sudden death throwing everyone into turmoil, can Rose unmask the killer stalking the corridors of Ridgewick Hall? And what of Rose's own secrets? Has the time come for a final reveal?

～

1

I woke to the sound of glass shattering followed by screaming.

I was out of bed and in the hallway before I even remembered where I was. After months away, travelling the world and reuniting with my cousins, I was back in London. In the home of Lord and Lady Ashton. Where someone was still screaming.

In the hallway, I ran into Alice, who was rubbing at her sleepy eyes and looking around for the source of the noises that had awoken her. "What was that noise? Who is screaming?"

I left her dazed and tired in her doorway and continued towards the sound. It was a female voice, probably my aunt or Catherine, but I couldn't tell which. And I didn't hear any sounds of a struggle or another voice. No obvious sign that someone unwelcome was in the house.

"Hello?" I called as I reached the end of the hall.

"Rose?" My aunt, Lady Ashton, ran up the stairs, eyes wide. "What is going on? I was in the kitchen, and—"

The screaming reached a new height and my aunt pushed past me with no regard for what kind of danger could be behind the door at the end of the hall and stepped inside. The room once belonged to her son Edward, the eldest cousin who was convicted of murder and then was murdered himself while in prison. He was the reason Catherine and Alice had briefly moved in with an aunt in New York City before ultimately returning home. The reason no one ever opened or discussed the room at the end of the hall. Lady Ashton, however, didn't seem concerned about it.

I followed her into the dark room, my eyes adjusting to the gloom, and found a figure standing in the corner. It was Catherine. She was still in her nightgown, her hair disheveled, and her eyes wide. She looked like a ghost, dressed in white with the faint light of the sunrise slipping through the closed curtain. A chill slid down my back at the sight, but my aunt, more concerned with her daughter than anything else, rushed into the room and grabbed Catherine by the shoulders.

"What is it, Catherine?" she asked, pulling her out of the corner and into the light.

Catherine grabbed her mother and pulled her close to her. "Careful."

Lady Ashton turned, looking around the room, and that was when I noticed the shattered glass in the middle of the floor. Lady Ashton had stepped over it to get to Catherine, but in backing up, she'd almost stepped on a large shard.

"The vases," Catherine said, her voice breaking in a sob. "Half of them are broken."

"The vases?" My aunt let go of Catherine and bent down to pick up a shard, studying it for a moment before turning back to her daughter. "You were screaming over a broken vase?"

"Six broken vases," Catherine corrected, running a hand down her head. "I told one of the decorators to put the vases upstairs and out of the way, and they must have put them in here."

Lady Ashton looked at me, eyebrows raised as if to ask if I could shed any light on the situation, and I just shrugged and shook my head. Now that I knew no one was in immediate danger, exhaustion had begun to take hold of my senses. Since being back in London, sleep had not come easily. When I'd left the city, I'd thought it would be for the last time. I'd imagined putting London and the Beckinghams behind me and stepping into a new life where I would not be forced to lie about who I truly was. Where I could create a new beginning for myself. Yet, only a few months later, I was back, and the transition had not been simple.

"They are for the garden party before the wedding," Catherine explained, near tears. "They will hold the fresh cut bouquets. I was lying in bed and realized I hadn't seen them with the other decorations, so I got up to look. I searched for two hours before finally looking in here, but the room is such a mess that I didn't see them behind the box, and I pushed it aside and broke everything."

The longer Catherine spoke, the more it became obvious she was exhausted and delirious. The stress of the wedding preparations had been weighing on her, making her already short temper even more volatile, but clearly, her sanity was now taking a turn.

"We can buy more vases, dear," Lady Ashton said, running a hand down Catherine's arm, soothing her the way I could imagine her doing when Catherine was just a child. "Six vases are nothing to be concerned about."

"There is already so much to do," Catherine lamented, sagging with the thought of another thing added to her list.

"Miss Brown will take care of it," Lady Ashton said with a wave of her hand, ending the discussion. "I'll send her out tomorrow to buy six more vases."

In the months since her son's murder conviction and then subsequent death, Lady Ashton had found her daily life significantly more difficult to bear. The press had grabbed hold of the sensational family drama and made it difficult for Lady Ashton to leave the house without being recognized. So, she'd hired yet another servant to handle those kinds of chores. The mousy-haired woman was only a few years older than me, but in the brief moments I'd seen her flitting from one chore to the next, she looked significantly older. I wondered whether it was simply her appearance or whether the wedding preparations were weighing heavily on her, as well.

"I brought these from New York. What if we cannot find any that match?" Catherine laid a hand over her forehead like she was feeling feverish, and I wouldn't have been surprised. I'd never seen her so unlike herself.

"Then we will buy them all brand new. Money is no matter." Lady Ashton coaxed Catherine from the corner like a trepidatious cat. "Now, go back to bed."

"What time is it?" Catherine said, a new wave of panic moving over her. "The designer will be here after breakfast to do a final fitting for my dress. Maybe I should just stay awake until—"

"No." Lady Ashton and I spoke at the same time, and Catherine looked at each of us carefully, eyes narrowed. For a moment, I thought she would take offense, but instead, she studied us and then sagged under her mother's arm and allowed herself to be led back to her bedroom.

I hadn't realized it, but Alice was standing outside the bedroom door during the entire conversation, and she watched Catherine walk past like she was afraid Catherine would strike out at her at any moment. When they were gone, she turned to me. "This wedding is driving her mad."

"She just needs a bit of sleep," I said, trying my best to defend my cousin, even though I was inclined to agree with Alice's assessment.

Alice pursed her lips, unconvinced. "A bit of sleep in an institution, perhaps. The woman is hysterical. She is getting married to a man she loves in a few days. Isn't she supposed to be happy?"

I laid a hand on Alice's back and encouraged her back down the hall towards her bedroom. "I suspect she will be once the wedding is over and she is married to Charles. Weddings can be very stressful."

Truly, I didn't know anything about weddings. I'd never had one nor attended one. The Beckinghams had been guests to several weddings while we lived in India, but the invitation never extended to me, which suited me perfectly fine. When the family left for an evening, it meant I would have the house to myself with no expectations of work. What I had gleaned from Catherine's wedding preparations, however, was that weddings were beautiful affairs mainly put on for the sake of the guests. Because from my vantage point, Catherine didn't seem to be enjoying herself. And Charles, who had agreed to return to London for the ceremony, seemed especially eager to return to his life in New York City. Especially now that his life in the city no longer involved being hunted by an assassin. Despite being in love, Catherine and Charles were not the picture of the blushing bride and groom-to-be I had always imagined. Catherine had been looking pale and thin for the better part of the last week, and now she was waking in the middle of the night to fret over vases. All of it seemed rather alarming.

Were I in her shoes, though, I imagined I would be in much the same state. In the week since we'd arrived in London and reclaimed our old rooms in the Ashton house, all manner of wedding planners, designers, and caterers had been in and out of the house. There seemed to always be someone who needed Catherine's attention. Questions about the centerpieces for the reception or the decorations around the church altar. Every question had to be run past Catherine before anything could move forward, so she hardly had time to sit and take a breath, let alone enjoy afternoon tea.

Lady Ashton, to her credit, had been doing her best to assist her daughter in whatever way she could, which mostly included being a host to the family members who decided to drop in and offer their congratulations before the actual ceremony. Cousins, aunts, and great aunts seemed to appear in greater and greater numbers every day, and they all expected to be served tea and finger snacks. Lady Ashton's personal attendant, Miss Brown, took on the responsibility of always having the sitting room tidy and ready for guests, despite the rest of the house having fallen into disarray.

I mostly felt as though I was in the way. Catherine had attempted to pass some of her responsibilities on to me, but when I failed to order the proper color table linens, she realized I would be of little use to her in the wedding planning, so whenever I asked, she insisted she did not need any help. If I had anywhere else to stay, I would have gone there in an instant. One more warm body in the house only added to the burden everyone else was carrying, but I sold my house in the city when I left with Achilles Prideaux with no intention of ever returning. My small room in the Ashton house—which had yet to be overrun by the wedding preparations that seemed to be filling the rest of the house, but I knew would be overtaken soon—was the only space in which I could be alone and out of everyone's hair. Alice's room, however, had been claimed by garment bags containing the many different dresses Catherine would be wearing over the week-long celebration. Alice made the logical point that the clothes could be kept in Catherine's room, but Lady Ashton wanted Catherine to have a quiet, tidy space to return to in the evenings, so her room was being kept clear of any preparations, which was why I suspected my room would be next.

After Catherine's screaming fit that woke up the

entire house, Alice went back to sleep for an hour before knocking on my door and entering without my permission.

"Why should her room be spared the chaos the rest of us are facing if she isn't even going to stay in there for an entire evening?" Alice asked, pacing around the room in her nightgown.

I'd tried several times to convince Alice to go back to her room, but much like her sister, she was in an irrational state, so I figured it would be a better use of my energy to sit in bed and hear her complaints out.

"Mother coddles her more than necessary. If Catherine were my daughter, I'd tell her to get a handle on herself and stop torturing everyone for the sake of one ceremony. Charles doesn't even seem to care about the wedding, so I'm not sure why it needs to be such an event."

"You did say that exact thing to Catherine over dinner last night," I reminded Alice. "You suggested she elope."

"Yes," Alice said, folding her hands behind her back and pacing over to the window, pulling the curtain back and scowling like she expected to see a wedding planner scaling the back wall to get inside. "But the advice would have carried more weight had my mother suggested it. At this point, it would be better for everyone if we didn't have to attend the wedding at all."

In New York City, Alice had been excited about the prospect of the wedding, drafting lists of which boys she would like to invite. However, upon returning to London, Lord Beckingham had quickly dashed those plans.

"There will be too many family and friends staying at

the estate to add another young man to the list," he said over breakfast our first full day back. "Besides, you will be helping your sister too much to worry about entertaining a young man."

Alice had argued valiantly, spending most of the day following her father and pestering him about his decision, but it held firm. No one, myself included, would be bringing along a date to the wedding. Since then, Alice's opinion on the whole matter had shifted quite dramatically.

"It is your sister's wedding. You want to be there to support her," I said, hoping it was true.

Alice's lip pulled up in the corner in disgust, and then she turned away from the window and dropped down on the end of my bed. Her short brown hair was unkempt, her untamed curls sticking out in every direction, making her look more like the young girl I'd first met a year ago than the woman she was quickly becoming.

"It seems my purpose in life is to follow Catherine and support her," she said bitterly. "I haven't seen my parents in months, and they have barely spoken to me except to correct me."

I leaned forward and tapped my finger against her nose affectionately. "Then do not give them so many reasons to correct you."

Alice rolled her eyes and opened her mouth to say something, probably to accuse me of being on everyone else's side, but before she could, the front bell rang. Alice's eyes shot wide and she stared at me. "Guests here before breakfast. Has everyone lost their minds?"

The guest in question was the designer of Catherine's

dress come to do final alterations before the final fitting. Catherine spent most of the morning standing on a small stool while the designer pinched and pulled on the fabric, pinning it down in places and telling her to stand tall and keep her shoulders back.

Family began to make their appearance just before lunch, all of them remarking on how gorgeous Catherine looked before glancing around the room in search of refreshments. One woman—middle-aged with graying blonde hair and a hearty appetite—took up a seat next to me throughout the morning, talking endlessly about family history and memories from her childhood.

"Your father and I, Rose, were close in age and, as children, found ourselves in all kinds of mischief." She went on to discuss their adventures climbing fruit trees behind Rose's grandmother's house and pulling childish pranks on a young Lord Ashton.

"I was heartbroken to hear about the accident," she concluded, shaking her head. "I'd made arrangements to visit you all in India not even a month later. Do you remember that?"

I remembered no such thing, but I nodded and smiled, thanking her for her sympathies and the fond memories. The moment she was gone, I turned to Alice. "I'm sorry, but who was that woman exactly?"

Alice had taken up the duty of informing me of who each family member was before they engaged me in conversation. Rose had not been in London for fourteen years before her death, so it was reasonable to expect her to not remember many of the Beckingham's distant family members. Yet, Alice had not whispered the middle-aged woman's name in my ear before she'd sat down, which had left me in the awkward position of foregoing her name throughout the entirety of our conversation.

Alice turned to me with her eyebrows pulled together. "I did not introduce her because I assumed you would know."

"I recognized her," I lied, a quiet kind of panic snaking up my neck. "But I could not recall her name."

A line of confusion formed across Alice's forehead as she spoke. "That was your father's cousin, Francis Atwater. Your family lived with her for a few weeks after selling your home here in London and before you left for India."

Fourteen years' time or not, Rose would have recognized Cousin Francis certainly. Alice's promptings had been so helpful to me over the last few days that I had forgotten to be on guard. I'd forgotten that I was still meant to be a member of this family.

"Oh, of course," I said with an embarrassed laugh. "How could I have forgotten her? Perhaps, the stress of the wedding has gotten to me, as well."

Alice smiled and nodded, but there was a hint of suspicion in her eyes. I resolved to not allow her to help me further. I would do my best to discover the names of Rose's relatives on my own.

2

The next morning, I rose even before the sun in an attempt to escape another day of wedding planning and family visits. The day before had made Alice suspicious, and I couldn't handle her watchful eye on top of my own anxiety. A day out of the house would do me good, and I knew Catherine would not miss me. However, despite my quiet sneaking around, I was stopped in the entrance hall by Alice's voice. I turned to see her standing on the stairs behind me.

"Where are you going so early?"

"A walk," I said quickly. "There is so little time for it during the day, and I haven't been out of doors as much as I'd like."

"I will come with you," Alice said at once, turning to run up the stairs. "I just need to change into my walking skirt and grab a hat."

"No." The word was harsh, and Alice stopped and turned, looking at me in confusion much as she had the day before. "You do not want my company?"

Alice was sensitive, never more so than in the last few days when so much of everyone's time and attention had been turned to Catherine. She felt left out by the others, and she would never forgive me if I did the same to her.

"It is not that," I said, scrambling to think of the proper excuse that would keep Alice from joining me and wouldn't incur any additional scrutiny.

Her eyes narrowed further, her head tilting to the side. "Are you meeting a man?"

I shook my head. "I am quite done with men for the moment."

Alice frowned sympathetically, nodding in understanding. The last man I'd kept in my company had proven to be a murderer and a liar. Alice felt the sting of his deception, as well, since she had taken a quick liking to him. The experience had had no effect on her feelings towards men, though.

"Then I do not see why I shouldn't come with you. I would also like to get out of the house, and if you aren't meeting a man, then there is no reason for privacy," she said, turning to move up the stairs.

Truly, I didn't know where I was going, but I wanted to be alone. Pretending to be Rose Beckingham had become easier over the last year, but it could still be taxing, and I knew the next days and weeks would only be more so. I needed time to myself.

"I am meeting a man," I lied, sagging my shoulders as though Alice had caught me in a lie.

She turned and let out a sharp laugh like she knew all along and had caught me. "I knew it. Who? Is it the detective?"

I almost forgot Alice and Catherine knew about my friendship with Achilles Prideaux. Neither knew that I had met with him twice in New York City, but they knew we had left together to work in Morocco. They also knew that I left him there to return to India. So, why Alice thought I would be going to meet him was a mystery. Probably, it was just that he was the only man she knew I was connected to.

"Yes," I said, deciding Achilles was better than creating some fictional man.

Her eyes lit up. "I will allow you to go alone if you promise to tell me everything about your meeting when you return."

I agreed to her conditions three times before she finally let me leave.

Summer mornings in London were brisk. The rising sun was still burning off the dew and fog, and the streets were free of people and cars. In direct opposition to the Ashton household, everything was quiet, which allowed me time to think about things I had not thought about since returning. And people.

The mention of Achilles Prideaux seemed to bring to life the part of my mind that had once fixated upon him. Seeing him in New York City, especially so unexpectedly, had been a shock. But a pleasant one. Time and distance had allowed me to mold my memory of him into an unflattering picture. I'd made his face sharper, his eyebrows more arched, and his personality harsher. Before seeing him, I'd assumed my memory served correct, but now that we had been reunited, and he had even gone so far as to help me uncover information about a case, I realized that I had been unkind to him.

Achilles' face was not rodentlike or sneaking. His cheeks had a pleasant, warm roundness, and the tan in his skin bespoke his world travels. His dark, thin mustache, which had once bothered me, seemed to suit his face well. His height should have made him gangly, but he was well-proportioned and moved with an air of grace most people could not emulate. And more than any of that, he was kind. After the way I'd left him so suddenly with no warning or explanation, Achilles should have never spoken to me again. He would have been well within his rights to turn up his nose at me and refuse to offer me any assistance. But not only did he go out of his way to assist me, he also warned me about my travelling companion before I ever suspected him of any wrongdoing. Despite everything I had done, Achilles still cared enough about my safety to keep a watchful eye on my movements and the company I kept. Surely, that meant part of him still cared for me the way he once had.

Inspired with hope, I stopped in a bank whose doors were open earlier than most and borrowed a pencil and scrap of paper from the teller. I scribbled a hasty note, thanked the woman, and then hurried down the street with a new sense of purpose.

Achilles' flat was not far from the Ashton's home, and I had made the trek often enough during my time in the city that I remembered it without hesitation. It was too early to knock on his door and demand his company. Besides, though I had found the courage to write him the note, I was not yet ready to address him face-to-face. I didn't know what I wanted to say or how I wanted to say it. I needed more time to think and plan, but one thing was certain: Achilles and I had unfinished business. So, I dropped the note through his mail slot and then hurried away before he could hear the noise and come to investigate.

MEET me at St. James's Park on Friday at 11. -Rose

I WALKED the streets aimlessly for the rest of the morning —no destination in mind except that I did not want to return to the Ashton home—until another fit of inspiration spurred me to hail a taxi and head to the North side of the city.

The morning was still new, but not too early for visitors, and certainly not too early for an old friend. And that was precisely what Mr. and Mrs. Worthing were to me after our adventures and correspondence together. Even when my travels took me from Morocco to India to America, I wrote to Mrs. Worthing and received letters from her frequently. When we disembarked from the ship that delivered us from Bombay to London almost a year before, I had no intentions of ever seeing the couple again, but I was surprised to realize what a large part of my life they had become. In truth, they were two of my only friends beyond my family and Achilles Prideaux— though his friendship had yet to be formally verified by the man himself.

When I knocked on Mr. and Mrs. Worthing's door,

none other than Aseem opened the door. The young Indian boy who had worked briefly as a servant in my own home had grown significantly in the last year. He seemed to be almost an entire head taller, now closer to my own height, and the softness of his chin had become squarer.

"Aseem," I said, both in delight and surprise before he could say anything.

His eyes widened before he regained composure of himself. "Miss Rose. What a surprise. Mrs. Worthing will be delighted by your visit." His voice was neutral, but his cheeks were rosy. It was nice to see that not everything had changed. He was still as quiet and outwardly unemotional as when I'd left.

"I'm here to see you, as well," I said, giving the young man a smile.

He stood a little taller at that and stepped aside, ushering me into a dark entryway.

It took a moment for my eyes to adjust to the gloom, but when they did, I saw Aseem dashing up the stairs, and moments later, a scream. For a second, I worried something had happened. Perhaps, a fall or a scare, but then I heard rapid footsteps and Mrs. Worthing appeared on the landing at the top of the stairs, arms outstretched for a hug even though we were an entire flight of stairs away from one another.

"Rose Beckingham," she said, her voice echoing off the marble floors. Aseem held out an arm to assist her, and Mrs. Worthing wrapped her arm through his, patting his forearm affectionately. Clearly, he had settled into their home well. "I did not know if you would ever find yourself in this part of the world again. I hoped, of course, but now, here you are."

I stepped forward and met her at the bottom of the stairs. Aseem moved aside and folded his hands behind his back patiently while Mrs. Worthing wrapped her arms around me and rocked us both slowly side to side while she hummed her enthusiasm.

"Dear, do not strangle the poor girl."

I opened my eyes, looking over Mrs. Worthing's shoulder to see Mr. Worthing at the top of the stairs. He had on trousers and a button-down shirt, but he was still in a housecoat and slippers, a cigar between his fingers.

"I won't," Mrs. Worthing replied, rolling her eyes. "But your cigar smoke might."

Mr. Worthing laughed like he was used to this joke and waved at me. "Good to see you again, Rose. Last we heard you were in New York City. What brings you back to London?"

Mrs. Worthing waved her arms to stop me from speaking. "We cannot talk in the doorway, Mr. Worthing. Rose, would you care to sit? Aseem makes a wonderful cup of spiced tea. A trick he learned in India, I have no doubt."

"I would love that," I said, smiling at the young boy who rushed off, happy to have a task to complete.

The sitting room was just as dark as the entryway, all of the blinds pulled despite the blue skies outside. The lamps cast the room in a yellow glow, and the fireplace was lit, the air warm and stuffy. It would have been a cozy space in the middle of winter, but it was a little overbearing for the summer. I took up the tufted armchair furthest from the flames.

"So," Mrs. Worthing said once she'd settled herself into the sofa and adjusted her throw pillows. "What brings you back to London, Rose? Last we heard, you were in New York City with your cousins. Awful news about their brother and his downfall in prison. I'm sure the time away from the city and the news was good for them."

Mr. Worthing elbowed his wife to caution her about her topic of choice, but she ignored him and gave me sad eyes, her lower lip pouting out. I almost smiled because the couple was exactly as I remembered them.

"I actually travelled back with Catherine and Alice, along with Catherine's fiancé," I said, grinning with the announcement. "Catherine's time in America was spent securing herself a husband."

Mrs. Worthing squealed and clapped her hands. "She is such a beautiful girl. Though, I am surprised you are not the one getting married, Rose. Catherine is lovely, but you have beauty and a personality to match. Not to say Catherine is not a nice girl, she is. It is just—"

"She can be intimidating," I said, cutting Mrs. Worthing off before she could say something she would regret.

"Exactly," she said, pointing at me. "Catherine can be intimidating, but you are such a dear. Do you think you will be married soon?"

"I'm afraid not," I said before thinking better of it. "Actually, to be frank, I'm not afraid. I'm not searching for love at all. Though, neither was Catherine and it found her, anyway."

My mind flickered back to the note I'd left in Achilles' mailbox only an hour before. That wasn't searching for love, though. A note didn't mean I loved him. It only meant I wanted to see him while I was back in the city. A friend calling upon a friend. Simple as that.

"That is a shame," Mrs. Worthing said. "Only because I do love attending a wedding."

"I haven't been to many," I admitted.

"Oh, they are wonderful," she said, reaching out to grab Mr. Worthing's hand. "Our wedding day was gorgeous. I've never felt as beautiful as I did wearing my dress."

She looked at her husband, eyes starry for a moment before they narrowed. I saw her softly nudge him. Mr. Worthing looked confused for a moment before he realized what he was supposed to say. "Oh no, dear. You've only grown more beautiful over the years."

Mrs. Worthing beamed, winked at her husband, and then turned back to me. "They are such enjoyable events, too. Reuniting with family and friends you haven't seen in awhile. Even meeting new friends."

"Catherine's wedding certainly seems like it will be an affair to remember." I began to explain the weeks of planning involved and the ever-increasing number of people who had been showing up to make the day run smoothly. "That is part of the reason I'm here, actually. I'm useless at this sort of thing, so it is better for me to be out of the house altogether."

"I'm sure that is not true," Mrs. Worthing said.

"I assure you it is." I laughed.

"Will the wedding be here in the city?" she asked.

"No, it will be in Somerset, actually."

Her smile faltered. "At the country house where we stayed for the weekend?"

I could see the unspoken part of the question in her eyes. *In the same house where a man was murdered in his sleep?*

"There will be a kind of celebration garden party in the garden there, but the ceremony itself will be held in the nearby village abbey."

She nodded and sighed in relief. "That sounds lovely. Lady Ashton has wonderful taste and is a fine host, so I'm sure it will be an affair to remember."

There was a hint of longing in her voice, and I knew what Mrs. Worthing wanted. More than anything, she liked to be included. Especially if the activity in question was any kind of party or celebration with a high-class crowd.

"Yes, it should be very nice," I said.

Thankfully, Aseem came in with a tray of tea and pastries just then, which served as a wonderful distraction. Mr. Worthing finally stubbed out his cigar in favor of a steaming cup of tea, and Mrs. Worthing insisted I take two pastries.

"You look so thin, Rose. All this travel has been hard on you, I think."

"I did not eat as well as I should have on the ship," I admitted.

"Will you be on another ship soon?" she asked. "It

seems you've spent the better part of the last year on one voyage or another."

"I'm not sure what my plan is next." This was true. I didn't have a plan. So far, the plans I'd made had fallen through in spectacular fashion, so it seemed more sensible to grab hold of whatever opportunities presented themselves and not think too far ahead at all. "I may be in London for awhile unless something else arises."

"I know I do not have a say in this, but I hope you'll stay for a time," Mrs. Worthing said. "I know we would all love your company. Aseem's reading has improved dramatically since you started writing to us. He reads every letter several times. He looks forward to your correspondence."

I turned to find Aseem blushing in the doorway, his eyes on the floor.

"I'm so glad to see your home has been a wonderful fit for Aseem. I hated the idea of leaving him without employment, so I'm overjoyed things have worked out so well."

"They have more than worked out," Mr. Worthing said. "In fact, if you do move back to the city, we may fight you over Aseem. I can't imagine our house running without him."

"I don't see that being a problem. I'm in no place to have another home here in the city anytime soon. Especially now that Catherine is getting married and moving back to New York, there will be plenty of room for me to take up my old room in my aunt and uncle's house."

"The country estate has plenty of space, too," Mrs.

Worthing said. "If the house here in the city ever became full. How many guests will be staying there for the wedding? I wager there will still be empty rooms available. It is a lavish estate."

Mr. Worthing was too busy enjoying his tea to give his wife the usual warning nudge.

"Actually, I believe it is full," I said. "Alice is devastated because she won't be able to invite a friend of hers to the wedding because there will be nowhere for him to stay."

Mrs. Worthing frowned and sighed. "I see."

Over the next hour, Mr. Worthing discussed the joys of retirement and Mrs. Worthing made three more references to being invited to the wedding.

"No offense towards Catherine or her intended, but after our last trip to Ridgewick Hall, I have no intention of ever returning," Mr. Worthing said.

Mrs. Worthing shot her husband an incredulous look. "Why do you say that?"

"A man died there," he pointed out. "We were unable to leave due to the investigation, and I still have nightmares about all of it. I'm happy to stay in the confines of my own home."

Based on the drawn curtains and musty air, I believed him wholeheartedly. I almost wished I could invite the Worthings just to spare them from their slightly oppressive house for a few days. But alas, I was in no position to be adding guests to Catherine's invite list, and truthfully, she would probably strangle me if she found out I was complicating the catering in any way.

Mrs. Worthing let the matter drop until we were once again standing in the entryway, preparing our goodbyes.

"Do not hesitate to drop in anytime," Mr. Worthing said warmly. "We welcome the company."

"Absolutely," Mrs. Worthing agreed. "We love company and parties and celebrations. We may look old, but we still have many good years of fun ahead of us."

Aseem made no move to step forward or wish me well, but he lifted his hand in a wave, and I smiled at him, confident the Worthings were a good fit. If there was anything I'd learned about Aseem during our time spent together, it was that he was as good at sneaking around as anyone I'd ever known. And the Worthings were hardly observant. My guess was that he found plenty of opportunities to sneak out of the stuffy old house and do as he wished without Mr. or Mrs. Worthing ever being the wiser.

"Certainly," I agreed. "I will visit again, hopefully with a good report from Catherine's wedding. I'll be sure to tell you all about it."

Mrs. Worthing smiled, but I could see the disappointment in the sinking of her shoulders. Before she could grow even bolder and ask for an invitation outright, I bid them all farewell and left.

3

When I returned to the Ashton's house after lunch, new family members had arrived: an older woman with the same square face and tan complexion as Lord Ashton and Mr. Beckingham and her three similar-looking daughters. The group of them ambushed me in the entryway as soon as I walked through the door, Miss Brown not far behind them.

"Lady Ashton will be back momentarily," Miss Brown said, looking frazzled. "She had to leave to help Miss Catherine with a wedding detail. But you are welcome to more tea."

"If I have any more tea, I'll burst," the older woman said. Then, she noticed me coming through the door. "Who are you?"

I opened my mouth to answer, but before I could, she shook her head. "I recognize you, Rose. You have grown since I last saw you."

My heart began to beat quickly. I looked around the

room, but there was no sign of Alice anywhere, and even if Alice was nearby, I didn't want to risk asking her for help. So, I stepped forward, a large smile spread across my face.

"It has been a long time, hasn't it?" I said, hoping the woman would reveal a useful piece of information.

"Almost fifteen years," she said with a curt nod. Then, she turned to her three daughters who were all standing in a quiet, tight line behind her, each of their shoulders touching. "And you remember Margaret, Anna, and Helen."

I nodded to the three girls, certain the woman in the middle was Anna, but being lost beyond that. Not only did the three women look unfamiliar, they all looked remarkably alike with medium-length brown hair twisted into a bun at the base of their necks, dark heavy brows, and slightly varying shades of the same pink sleeveless drop-waist dress.

"Is there anything I can get you, Mrs. Blake?" Miss Brown asked.

"We came here to spend time with family," the woman, whose surname was apparently Blake, said. "And now that my niece has arrived, I'm sure she can take on the hosting duties."

Aunt. "Yes, absolutely, Aunt," I said, turning then to the women behind her. "Cousins. Follow me. Catherine has been so busy this week, but I am so pleased to see you all. It has been far too long."

"I'd hoped to see you at the funeral for my brother," Mrs. Blake said.

"Oh, yes. I wish things had worked out differently. Unfortunately, due to the accident, I wasn't in a good place to plan anything, so nothing was arranged aside from a quiet burial."

She pursed her lips and then shrugged. "William never was one for formalities, was he? I suppose he would enjoy a quiet burial. Though, to my understanding, there were not enough remains for an actual burial."

I nodded solemnly, surprised by the blunt way she referred to her brother's gruesome death. "Correct. The grave marker is just there to mark their memory."

Suddenly, out of nowhere, there was a sharp bark of laughter. I jumped and turned to see one of the three daughters was laughing. "Rose, do you remember the prank we convinced you to pull during the Christmas dinner when you were only six or seven?"

I stammered, hoping the woman would carry on with the story without any response from me, but it appeared that would not happen. "No, I actually can't recall."

"Rose took part in a prank?" I turned to see Alice standing in the doorway. "I can't imagine it. Is it true, Aunt Ruth?"

Aunt Ruth. I committed the name to memory, grateful for Alice's arrival already. Aunt Ruth nodded, though she didn't look as pleased at the memory as her daughters did. "Rose was always a mischievous child. I warned William that he should take sharper control of her, but it seems she turned out fine despite him never taking my advice."

The same daughter who spoke before continued the

story. "Everyone was gathered at Ashton House for Christmas dinner, and we snuck into the kitchen where Anna lifted Rose up to the counter—"

"I thought it was Margaret," Aunt Ruth said, looking to me.

The daughter speaking, who I now knew had to be Helen, turned to me, as well. "Do you remember, Rose?"

I pointed to the daughter sitting to the right of Helen, who I'd decided in the entryway was Anna. "I think Helen is right. It was Anna."

The sister to the left of Helen shifted nervously in her seat. "I'm Anna."

My face flamed, and I shook my head, laughing nervously. "I'm sorry. It has apparently been far too long. Of course, you are Anna."

I studied each of their faces, searching for the key differences that would help me tell them apart later, but I couldn't find any. Were they identical triplets? So, I remembered their gowns. Anna wore the lightest shade of pink, Helen was in the darker shade, and Margaret's perfectly matched the color of her skin and was quite unflattering. The trick would only last until the women changed their clothes, but it was better than nothing. I didn't turn around, but I could feel Alice's eyes on me. I wished she was the same silly young girl she'd been when I'd first arrived in the city. That Alice would have been too busy offering fashion advice and asking the women if they were married or had any suitors to pay attention to me.

Helen waved her hands to dismiss the matter and

carried on. "Either way, we lifted little Rose up to the counter and had her replace the sugar bowl with salt."

The three women all began laughing hysterically, grabbing onto one another like it was the funniest thing they had ever heard, and I did my best to join in.

"What happened then?" Alice asked, smiling widely and moving to sit on the sofa next to me.

The three women were still laughing, so Alice turned to me. I wanted to pick up the story and continue it the way Rose would. It was no doubt a family story that would be retold whenever family members got together. Even if Rose didn't remember the act of doing it, she would have heard the tale. But I was drawing a blank. I'd never heard Rose tell the story or Mr. Beckingham mention it.

Alice raised her eyebrows, encouraging me to continue, and I stared blankly back at her.

"Well," Helen finally said, controlling herself enough to speak. Alice mercifully turned her attention to her other cousin, and I sagged with relief. "The dish was taken out with tea service and everyone made their cup, but Uncle James, as I'm sure you know Alice, enjoys a lot of sugar in his tea."

Alice's mouth opened wide, delighted. "He does. Mama says it is obscene."

"He put several spoonfuls of what he thought was sugar in his cup, and when he took a drink—" Helen fell into another fit of giggles, clutching her stomach, and Alice turned back to me.

I looked helplessly at the three sisters, hoping one of

them would break out of their laughter long enough to finish the story, but they were gone.

"What happened?" Alice pleaded, smiling in anticipation.

"He spit it everywhere," Aunt Ruth said quickly. "He spit the drink out and drenched William. The part of the story the girls are all forgetting is that they spent the rest of the evening sitting in the corner instead of eating dessert."

Margaret wiped the tears from her eyes and smiled. "It was well worth it. Almost twenty years later, and I'm still laughing. I can't believe you forgot, Rose. It is one of my favorite childhood memories."

"I remember more now that you explained it," I said, lying completely. Then, I stood, smoothing down the front of my linen dress. "If you will all excuse me, though, I need to freshen up. I've been running around this morning."

Alice moved to follow me, no doubt eager to ask how my fictitious meeting with Achilles Prideaux went, but before she could, Aunt Ruth stopped her to ask brusquely about her time in New York City and whether it was educational.

The moment I walked into my room, I pressed myself against the door and took a deep breath. I couldn't decide if I was paranoid or if Alice truly was noticing something strange about my behavior. It didn't help that every interaction felt like a test. Each new family member who walked through the doors of the Ashton household was a hurdle I had to overcome. Was I supposed to know them or not? Were they from my side of the family or Lady

Ashton's? The stress of it was piling on my shoulders, and I felt like I was being pushed further and further into the ground.

Since making the decision to take on Rose Beckingham's identity, I'd faced the possibility that I would one day have to tell her family—the people who I had come to view as my own beloved family—the truth about my deception. I did not imagine, however, that they would uncover my lie because of my own inability to maintain my disguise. It was a terrifying reality, and one I was not sure I was ready to contemplate.

I used the time in my room to change out of my walking clothes and into a green silk and chiffon dress, apply a bit more powder to the scar on my cheek—a lasting reminder of the bombing that began the entire mess, and regain my composure. Soon enough, everyone would be at Ridgewick Hall. The grounds of the family estate were expansive, and no one would notice if I slipped away during the day and spent more of my time alone. And if anyone did comment on my disappearances, I could explain that seeing so many family members together reminded me that my own parents would not ever arrive. It wouldn't be too far from the truth. Playing the role of Rose Beckingham in front of so many relatives left me uneasy, guilt gnawing at me constantly.

When I returned to the sitting room, Catherine and Lady Ashton had finished whatever wedding preparations they had been taking part in, so I was free to sit back and observe rather than take an active role in the conversation. It was a welcome change of pace. And when Lord

Ashton arrived home from his club, he and Ruth spent the evening reminiscing about their childhood. Though, their reminiscences lacked the laughter and smiles one would expect. Together, they were direct and straightforward as though they were being interrogated about their memories.

THE NEXT DAY, in an effort to avoid Aunt Ruth and her daughters, I begged Catherine to let me assist her with the wedding plans.

"I can run an errand for you," I offered, trying my best not to sound as desperate as I felt. "Anything you need done today, just tell me. I can handle it."

Catherine worried with her lower lip, biting the already red and raw skin. "I think everything is being handled, Rose."

When I'd walked in the room, I'd heard Catherine lament to Lady Ashton that there was no way everything would be done in time for the wedding. I narrowed my eyes at her. "We leave for Ridgewick tomorrow. This is your last day to finalize plans and pack. Are you certain you don't need any help?"

I could see the anxiety rising behind Catherine's eyes. She was teetering on the precipice of another breakdown, and I was willing to nudge her closer to the fall if it meant I had an excuse to be away from the house.

"Rose could buy new vases," Lady Ashton said, her finger running down what looked to be a long list of tasks that still needed to be completed. "Miss Brown went to look for six more yesterday but could not find any replacements. So, we will need to buy twelve new ones."

Catherine turned and gave her mother a sharp look, but Lady Ashton waved away her daughter's worries with a smile. "Rose can handle it. Can't you, Rose?"

"Absolutely," I agreed, happy to have a task even if it was against Catherine's wishes. "What should the vases look like?"

The next ten minutes were passed listening to Catherine describe a white vase with flowers etched down the sides in excruciating detail. She even tried to convince me I needed to take one of the original vases she'd purchased in New York City with me as an example.

"I can remember what it looks like," I said, only slightly offended she had so little faith in me.

As I left, I heard Lady Ashton comforting her daughter. "The vases are only for the garden party, dear. If they are wrong, at least it won't affect the wedding."

I was tempted to come home with eleven black vases just as punishment for their bad faith, but my pride wouldn't allow it. I may not have had the same kind of experience in planning parties and events as Lady Ashton and Catherine, but I could manage buying twelve vases.

Alice caught me by the elbow on my way out of the house, her eyes wide and eager. "Where are you going? Can I come with you?"

I knew if I denied her request outright, it would only increase her desire to go. So, I shrugged. "If you'd like. I am on a mission to buy vases for the wedding."

Her desire faded at once, her eyes and shoulders drooping. "Is this wedding all anyone can talk about? I'd rather stay here and listen to Aunt Ruth and father talk about stocks. They've been talking of nothing else all morning. So dull."

"I will offer you more lively company when I return?" I suggested.

Alice grabbed my hand, made me swear I'd save her from the clutches of her dull aunt and strange cousins, and then sulked into the sitting room.

I went to three different shops before I found the perfect vases. In fact, they were near replicas of the vases Catherine had purchased in New York City. Had it been my wedding, I would have deemed them a close enough approximation and only purchased six to replace the broken ones, but I knew there was no such thing as "close enough" when it came to Catherine and her wedding planning. Every detail had to be just right, including the vases that would hold the fresh cut flowers from the family's well-kept garden.

The shop owner was pleased to make such a large sale and promised me the vases would be wrapped, packaged carefully, and delivered to the Ashton household later that afternoon. I thanked him and then stepped out onto the street. I wanted to rush home to prove to Catherine that the task had not only been managed, but managed in a timely fashion. I'd found exactly what she wanted in less than two hours. However, I had other plans.

The taxi let me out in front of Buckingham Palace. Visitors to London and locals were gathered around the exterior gates, eager for a glimpse of a member of the royal family or to see the changing of the guard. I walked in the opposite direction, however, towards the gates of St. James's Park.

The walking path was wide, small fences on either side keeping back the grass and foliage of the well-maintained garden. Trees hung over the path, offering shade even in the midday sun, and I did my best to keep my pace even, my stroll casual. I didn't know where Achilles Prideaux would be.

My note had been vague. Just a location and a place. Knowing the detective, he would show up early and watch from a distance in order to understand the circumstances of the meeting. After everything we'd been through, I could never blame him for being suspicious. Knowing that about him, I didn't want to appear overeager or nervous. I wanted to look like a woman on her way to meet an old friend. No other motives or purpose.

I dressed nicer than a day running errands for Catherine called for. My dusty rose dress was silk with a layer of dyed lace over the top. The dropped waist had crepe flowers on the hip, and I wore a matching lace headband with a flower over my left ear. Achilles noticed small details, and I wanted to give him plenty to notice.

I had never worried about such things before, especially when it came to Achilles. Especially once he revealed he had known I was not truly Rose Beckingham from the day we met. I never had to pretend to be anyone or anything I was not with him, but after seeing him in New York City, my feelings had shifted. A nervousness I'd never felt around him or anyone else twisted my insides and made me feel light-headed.

I wasn't naïve enough to think I could actually be ill, but it certainly felt that way. As I walked deeper into the park, the walkway curving over to run alongside the water, I considered turning around and leaving. It would be simpler to go back to the Ashton house, leave with the family for Ridgewick Hall, and forget about Achilles Prideaux. But I knew that would do nothing to stop the thoughts I'd been having. If I wanted this issue resolved, I had to speak with Achilles. I had to understand what our relationship would look like moving forward. It was the only way I'd ever have any kind of closure.

So, I claimed an empty bench near the edge of the water, a family of ducks and ducklings splashing along the bank, and waited.

Every time anyone walked past the bench, I looked up. I told myself not to—that Achilles would find me when he was ready—but as minutes slipped by without any sign of him, I couldn't stop myself. Perhaps, I should have given him a specific location within the park to meet me. Perhaps, I should have knocked on his door that morning I left the note and spoken to him in person instead. Maybe the note had slipped under a piece of furniture and he never received it. Or, just as likely, maybe he saw the note and decided not to come.

I'd hoped we were close enough that he would send me a note telling me he would not be meeting me, but I couldn't say for sure. And the longer I sat on the bench waiting for him, the less sure I became of everything.

For a time, I tried to convince myself I had simply

arrived early. I fed the ducks that came up onto the path to eat the small pieces of bread I'd brought with me and did my best not to focus on the time. However, when the clock tower rang noon, any lingering hopes I had were dashed.

Achilles Prideaux was not coming.

4

When I arrived back at the Ashton household, the excited shop owner had just delivered the vases several hours earlier than he said and Catherine was cutting into the box to inspect them. She was so busy pulling back the lid and digging through the wrapping paper, that she didn't hear me come in behind her. I held my breath as she pulled out one of the vases and held it up, studying it from every angle.

"These will work fine," she said, surprise obvious in her voice.

I knew that was the most praise I'd receive, and it was good enough for me. Honestly, the vases and Catherine's opinion of them meant less to me than they had that morning. As we gathered for lunch and listened to Catherine and Lady Ashton discuss everything left to prepare before we left for Ridgewick Hall, I couldn't focus on anything other than Achilles Prideaux.

Should I write him another letter asking why he

hadn't met me at the park? Should I go directly to his house so as not to give him the time to formulate a fictitious excuse? What had changed from New York City when he had been willing to assist me with a case to now when he wouldn't even meet me?

Apparently, my distraction was obvious because Catherine found me in my room after lunch. She knocked on the door, and I expected it to be Alice, eager to collect on my earlier promise of keeping her company.

"Oh," I said, surprised.

"Expecting someone else?" she teased, pushing open the door and stepping inside. "Perhaps, the person who has made you so morose?"

"Am I morose?" I asked, sitting on the edge of my bed, fingering the delicate fabric of my dress.

Catherine nodded. "All afternoon. I've been distracted lately, but we have become friends over these last few months, and I couldn't allow you to be sad over what is supposed to be a happy weekend."

She moved to sit next to me on the bed and laid her hand over mine. "What is wrong?"

If the wound hadn't been so fresh, I may have resisted. I may have kept the hurt to myself so as not to dampen Catherine's own happiness in any way. But as it was, I told her immediately. I explained my meeting with Achilles Prideaux in New York City. I told her about our friendship—leaving out the part about him knowing my true identity—and explained that, for me, it had grown into something more.

"Clearly, he does not feel the same way," I said, cheeks

flushing with embarrassment. "It is silly to be upset over something like this, but—"

"Silly?" Catherine shook her head. "Love is one of the only reasons to be upset, cousin. If I've learned anything over the last year, it is that love is what matters. Love for your family, your friends...romantic love. Everything else is fleeting, but love remains."

"How poetic of you," I teased, managing a small smile.

Catherine nudged me with her shoulder. "It is true. If you love this man, then you have every right to be upset." She got quiet and pulled her hand away from mine, setting it on her own lap instead. "But would you really want to marry a detective, anyway?"

The idea of marrying Achilles had never crossed my mind, and suddenly it all sounded quite ridiculous. The two of us married? I couldn't think of a more ridiculous image. And yet, I could still see it. I would wear a lace dress. White, of course.

"I'm not sure about marriage," I said. "But I do like him."

Catherine shrugged. "It is just that you two would be so similar. Charles and I work well because we are very different. You may not have noticed, but he is softer than I am. Gentler."

I had, in fact, noticed, but I didn't know how to say so without offending Catherine. "So, you think I need a gentle man? One like Charles?"

"I won't claim to know what you need."

I turned to her with my eyebrow arched. "That is the most surprising string of words I think I've ever heard."

She nudged me again, pursing her lips to hide a laugh. "I only mean that if this Achilles Prideaux would make you happy, then I do not wish to discourage it. I just think it would be wise to test your love before committing to the idea of him. Sometimes, we want things that are not good for us. After everything you have been through, I only want you to have what is good for you."

Between the disappointment of my failed meeting with Monsieur Prideaux and Catherine's kindness, my well of emotions was overflowing. Tears pricked the backs of my eyes, and I swallowed back against the display of emotions.

In a way, it was easier when Catherine disliked me. It made my deception easier to bear. As the family has warmed to me, though, their kindness had increased my guilt several fold. When Catherine was kind to me, I couldn't help but wonder if she would extend the same kindness if she knew the truth. If she knew that I was not truly her cousin. Would she still only want what was good for me? I wagered not.

Luckily, before Catherine could catch on to my emotional display, the door to my room burst open and Alice rushed in, looking near tears herself.

"Alice!" Catherine reprimanded, pressing a hand to her chest. "You shouldn't barge into rooms like that. Do you want to frighten me to death before my wedding?"

"You two never include me," Alice said, crossing her arms. She turned to me, her brown eyes narrowed. "I've asked you about Achilles several times, and you never opened up to me. I might be younger than you, but I have enough experience to listen and offer advice. Unlike

Catherine, I think you should go straight to Achilles' house now. You should ask him why he did not show up to your meeting."

"Alice." Catherine stood up, arms crossed like a blond, mirror image of her younger sister. "Just because you think you ought to be privy to the private details of everyone else's life does not give you any right to go skulking around the house with your ear pressed to the door."

Alice's cheeks flushed. "I didn't have to press my ear to the door."

"Regardless," Catherine said. "You cannot behave this way during my wedding. We will have guests staying at the country estate with us, and I don't want them to worry that their private affairs will be made public."

"Oh, I don't care about the private matters of Aunt Ruth and her daughters. They are so dull," she said. "But I shouldn't have had to listen outside the door, anyway. Rose promised she would talk to me about everything when she returned, but she didn't."

Catherine opened her mouth to reprimand her sister further, but I stood up and crossed the room before she could, taking Alice by the hands and pulling her towards the bed. "You are right, Alice. I should have kept my promise. The truth is, I'd hoped to come to you with better news about my meeting, but when Achilles didn't show up, I was embarrassed. I didn't plan to tell anyone about it, but Catherine got the truth out of me."

Alice's lips twisted to the side as she sat on the bed next to me, Catherine on my other side. "If it helps at all, I think Achilles Prideaux must be a remarkably dumb man. No intelligent man would leave Rose Beckingham waiting."

A rush of guilt rose up in me like the ocean against a sea wall, and I had to fight to remain steady. To keep hold of my identity as Rose Beckingham.

"Thank you, Alice. Unfortunately, he is a very intelligent man, though I appreciate the sentiment." I squeezed her hand and then turned to Catherine. "But enough about my disappointment. Your wedding is days away, Catherine. Are you excited?"

Catherine smiled, though it was weary. "Is it wrong to admit I'm most anxious about being done with the planning?"

"No," Alice said quickly. "I can't wait to have my room back."

Catherine rolled her eyes and continued. "I have loved being back in London, but I'm anxious to return to our life in New York. And I know Charles is, as well. He misses his friends and his work. I've been so busy with the wedding that we have hardly seen one another since we've returned."

"You will have more than enough time to see one another once you are married," I reminded her. "A lifetime."

Alice made a kind of gagging noise in the back of her throat, but pretended it was a cough when Catherine shot her a violent look.

"I never would have thought I'd live in New York City," she said thoughtfully. "I always imagined I'd stay in London forever. And now, here I sit, anxious to return to America. Life can be funny, can't it?"

I wanted to express to Catherine exactly how much I understood her. One event had set my life on an entirely new path I never would have dreamed of. Without the bombing and claiming Rose's identity, I never would have met Catherine and Alice. I never would have met Achilles, either. I'd probably still be in India, working for another family as a household servant.

"You wouldn't have even met Charles had it not been for Edward," Alice said.

Immediately, Catherine stilled next to me. Alice pressed her lips together nervously, realizing what she had said. There was no rule against mentioning Edward, but it was rarely done. It had been many months since his crime and subsequent murder in prison, but the wounds were still fresh for his family. His absence was felt keenly, especially now that everyone was together under the same roof again.

"Sorry," Alice mumbled. "I didn't mean—"

"No, it's all right," Catherine said, giving her younger sister a small smile. "You are right. Had Edward not... done what he did...we never would have gone to New York City to stay with Aunt Sarah, and I never would have met Charles. Good or bad, life finds a way to work out."

We were all quiet for a moment, and then Alice sighed. "It will be strange to return to Ridgewick without Edward. We've never gone without him before."

Catherine nodded in agreement. "Strange, indeed."

I sat between them, still and quiet, unsure what to say or whether I needed to say anything at all. I'd hardly known Edward, and our time together had not been pleasant in the least. Thankfully, the mood shifted back to happier thoughts without my assistance when Alice brought up that Charles Barry would be at the wedding.

"He was so in love with you last time we visited he could hardly stand it," Alice teased, leaning around me to pinch her sister's arm.

Catherine blushed. "I'm about to be a married woman, Alice."

"I know," Alice said, a wicked smile playing on her lips. "Perhaps, he will settle for the younger Beckingham."

Catherine snorted. "If you can pull him from the company of his sister long enough for him to notice you, that is. Those two are stitched at the hip."

Soon, the conversation devolved into fits of laughter about the guests and the festivities to come, and Edward and Achilles slipped from our minds entirely.

5

Moving the entire family, staff, and necessary supplies for Catherine's wedding from London to Ridgewick was a grueling experience. Miss Brown and George, the driver, oversaw the packing, but Catherine was so concerned about her dress being ruined or the decorations being crushed that she personally walked each box of supplies from the house to the car. Lady Ashton tried in vain to settle her eldest daughter, and the only thing that would calm Catherine was calling on Charles Cresswell, her betrothed, to come to the house and sit with her while things were loaded and prepared.

My duty was to keep Alice away from Catherine. Though the two shared a moment of sisterly bonding the day before, the stress of moving to the country estate set them on one another. Each time Catherine would pass by Alice's perch on the stairs, Alice would make some comment under her breath about the horrible demise that was sure to befall the entire wedding if Catherine didn't personally oversee every single incompetent servant. By the third trip, Catherine was angry enough to forget all propriety and kick Alice, nearly knocking her down the stairs. So, to avoid another murder in the family, I kept Alice busy with gossip about the boys she'd met since returning to London and (mostly fictional) tales of my own romantic escapades in India.

Once the party made it to Ridgewick Hall, everyone was so busy unloading the cars, preparing the house, and greeting the guests who managed to arrive at the estate before Lord and Lady Ashton much to Lady Ashton's dismay that there was no time for Alice and Catherine to fight or for me to keep them apart even if I wanted to.

"Rose," Lady Ashton asked, pulling me aside soon after our arrival. "Would you kindly keep Aunt Augusta company?"

I frowned, looking around to decide which of the guests milling the grounds was Aunt Augusta, but Lady Ashton mistook my expression for disappointment.

"I know, she is a horrible woman," she said. I'd rarely heard Lady Ashton say an unkind word about anyone. "But keeping Catherine from worrying herself to death is a full-time chore, and I can't trust Alice not to say something inappropriate, and Miss Brown—"

"I am glad to do it," I said, interrupting my aunt's tirade.

She sighed in relief, pulled me into a quick hug, and hurried off to stop Catherine from carrying in the large box of vases by herself.

Servants and distant relations were scattered across the large front garden of Ridgewick Hall, admiring the architecture of the three-story stone building and the landscaping, and not one of them looked familiar to me. There was an elderly man with a bald spot on the back of his head and the rest of his hair swirling around it like a gray bird's nest, who I could firmly rule out as being an aunt, but otherwise, there were no clues. So, I walked up the wide, shallow stairs that led to the front porch and waited for the woman to make herself known. After fifteen minutes of that, I gave up and pulled Alice aside.

"Where is Aunt Augusta?" I whispered. "Your mother wants me to keep her busy, but I don't recall who she is."

"I don't see how it could be possible to forget her," Alice groaned, adjusting the lace collar of her pale pink dress. "Miserable old woman. I haven't seen her yet, but I can help you find her."

Lady Ashton seemed to think it would be wise to keep Alice away from Aunt Augusta, but if she was truly as horrible as everyone claimed, perhaps Alice's company would help. So, Alice linked her arm through mine and we walked down the stone path that ran the perimeter of the estate.

The house was a beautiful, yet imposing structure. It seemed to hulk over everything, casting long shadows across the grass, but the delicate vine and flower details carved into the stone around the windows and the doors offset its domineering structure slightly. The ground had the same dichotomy. Ancient trees towered over the home and shaded large portions of the grass, but sunlight shone through the leaves and branches, creating a lace-work of light across the ground. Everything was dappled in delicate sunshine.

As we rounded the back corner of the estate, the pathway moved east, cut through an outcrop of trees, and wrapped around the far end of the property. A well-manicured garden blooming with thick hydrangea bushes and lavender surrounded a circular pond. There, next to the pond, stood a broad-shouldered man with dark hair peeking from beneath his derby hat. Next to him was an elderly woman with a severe slash of white hair on her head and an angular, skeletal face. Alice stopped walking and grabbed my hand, jerking me backwards.

"Who is that?" she asked, pointing to the pair.

"That is why I brought you," I said. "I haven't the faintest idea."

"Well, the woman is Aunt Augusta, obviously," she said. "But the man next to her. I've never seen him before."

"Then, I don't know why you expected me to recognize him," I teased, but Alice was too far lost in her admiration of the young man to notice.

I followed her gaze and had to admit he was handsome. Heavy, thoughtful brows, a straight nose, and plump lips visible even from a distance. He could easily have been mistaken for a lifelike statue rather than a real man, which was precisely why I did not appreciate him the way Alice did. He was almost too handsome.

Sensing our appraisal, the man looked over, and Alice jumped behind me to shield herself.

I pulled my cousin's arm and brought her to my side once again. "We have to go over there. He has seen us staring, and now it will be rude if we do not make introductions."

Alice's face went pale. "Perhaps, I should go and assist Catherine. She will be wanting my help."

"Catherine wants no such thing," I said, gripping her hand tightly, refusing to let her flee. She pulled so hard against my restraint that her cloche hat went askew. "This man is likely a relative of yours, and you are being rude."

This revelation stilled her struggles to escape. "Do you think he is a relative?"

"Everyone here is a relative," I reminded her. "It is a family wedding."

I could not tell if this information calmed or upset her, but it made her thoughtful enough that I was able to cross the lawn and approach the unlikely pair.

"Aunt Augusta," I said, greeting the old woman as if I knew her at once. "It is so wonderful to see you."

The old woman turned to me, her thin upper lip tensed in obvious displeasure, and said nothing. She wore a dark navy dress with long sleeves and stockings. She had to be sweltering in the heat, though there was no sign of sweat gathering on her forehead or anywhere else.

I blinked several times, waiting for someone to say something to end the silence, but Alice was frozen at my side, staring at the man next to Aunt Augusta, and Aunt Augusta was staring at me. Desperately, I turned to the man at her side and smiled.

"I'm sorry. I'm not sure if we have ever met. I am Rose Beckingham." I extended a hand which he grabbed at once. "And this is my cousin, Alice. The younger sister of the bride."

Alice's hand seemed to float away from her body, and

her eyes went wide when the man took her hand and shook it.

"I recognize your names, though not the faces," he said warmly. "We are so happy to be here for such a joyous occasion."

Aunt Augusta sniffed suddenly in such a way that I could not tell if she was ill or snorting in disagreement. Everyone chose to ignore her.

"And who are you?" Alice asked, finally finding her voice.

"Nicholas," he said. "Nicholas Whitlock."

"My grandson," Aunt Augusta said coldly, her voice faint and hoarse. She paired her unfriendly words with a familiar squeeze of Nicholas' arm.

"Grandson," Alice repeated. I could see her drawing the family tree in her head, trying to see what that made Nicholas to her.

"He is your second cousin," I offered helpfully. "On Lady Ashton's side, I suspect?"

Nicholas nodded. "Are you part of the Whitlock side, or—?"

"No, my father was Lord Ashton's brother."

"So, the two of you are not related?" Alice said, glaring up at me with an intense jealousy.

I laughed awkwardly. "We are all family this weekend. It is wonderful to meet you, Nicholas."

"Your parents died," Aunt Augusta said, narrowing her milky eyes at me. His skin was pale and papery. I expected it to tear when a gentle breeze blew over the grounds. "The bombing. Remember, Nicholas?"

Nicholas' jaw clenched, and he smiled down at his

grandmother. "Yes, I do remember hearing about that." He turned to me, eyes apologetic. "Terrible tragedy. My condolences."

I smiled and tipped my head, fearing I would be discussing the tragedy that had befallen the Beckingham family repeatedly over the course of the weekend.

"That is where you got the scar." Aunt Augusta continued, pointing to her own cheek with a shaky hand. It was not a question, simply a statement.

My fingers fluttered nervously to the dent in my left cheek. So few people had addressed my injury outright that I could almost forget it was there. "Um, yes," I stammered. "It is."

Nicholas wrapped an arm around his grandmother's shoulders. "I live with my grandmother full-time. Caring for her needs and keeping her company."

"Full-time?" Alice asked. I knew at once we had the same thought about the situation. Why would anyone agree to that?

"I am growing old, but I am not yet ill enough to require constant care," Aunt Augusta said sharply. "Though, I do appreciate the company. Especially after the break-in last month."

I turned to Nicholas. "Someone broke into your house?"

"Well," he started, shrugging as if he wasn't sure how to explain it.

"Yes, they did," Aunt Augusta said, interrupting Nicholas' explanation. "The police are investigating the matter now, but the criminals will likely never be caught.

These kinds of crimes are often neglected, especially when an old woman is the target."

"There is no proof anyone was ever in the house, Grandmother. You didn't actually see anyone, so the police don't even have a description to work from."

"Just because I did not see them doesn't mean it didn't happen," she said. "Some of my finest silver was taken from a shelf in the dining room and a painting is missing from the attic. Of course, the most important thing stolen was my peace of mind."

"I know," Nicholas said like he'd heard the story retold many times. He rubbed his grandmother's shoulders. "But we had been cleaning and reorganizing. Perhaps, those things were taken out with the trash by mistake."

Aunt Augusta shook her head, dismissing the idea. "No. I know what happened. Someone came into my home and stole from me."

She turned her gaze on me, narrowing her eyes as though I could have been the one to steal from her, and I realized Lady Ashton's request would be more difficult to fulfill than I thought.

"Would you care for a walk around the grounds?" I asked. "It is a beautiful day."

Nicholas smiled and nodded, but before he could say anything, Aunt Augusta curled her lip and shook her head. "I'd like to go up to my room. I'm chilled to my bones and would do much better with a blanket."

Without hesitation, Nicholas bid us farewell and slowly walked his grandmother towards the house.

The moment they were out of earshot, Alice sighed. "I

heard Aunt Augusta had a grandchild taking care of her, but it is unforgivable to keep someone that handsome locked away in her mansion."

"Locked away?" I whispered. "What do you mean?"

"Aunt Augusta is almost a shut-in," she said, narrowing her eyes. "How could you have never heard of her situation?"

"She isn't technically my family."

Alice shrugged. "I suppose she isn't, but it is still surprising. She is by far the wealthiest person on our side of the family, but she rarely leaves her home. She keeps very few servants and has accused everyone she knows of stealing from her twice. Her accusations are unfounded, of course. Many believe the money has cost her sanity."

"Perhaps, you are being too harsh on the old woman, Alice. She seems to trust Nicholas, and she left her home in London to come all the way to Somerset."

Alice shook her head. "You'll see. Ask anyone. No one likes her."

We turned and walked down the path in the direction we'd come from, moving back towards the front of the house. "That doesn't seem like appropriate party conversation. *Excuse me, do you think Aunt Augusta is a suspicious shut-in?*"

She laughed. "Maybe not, but I'll save you the trouble. Yes, she is."

When we got back to the front of the house, several more cars had parked in the circular driveway, and Lady Ashton was answering questions from the servants while greeting guests. Lord Ashton had taken up a conversation with several other men in the front corner of the garden, but it did little to ease my aunt's burden. So, with Alice by my side, we welcomed people to the estate and ushered them up the long walkway to the front doors of the house. Alice had to remind me of everyone's names, whispering them in my ear as they approached.

Finally, the deluge of guests began to wane, and Alice grabbed my arms and pulled me up the walkway towards the house.

"If we do not leave now, I'm afraid we'll never be free," she whispered. "I expected this time in the country to be relaxing, but how am I to relax if we are being treated as servants?"

"We are the hosts. It is expected that we should help make the guests comfortable."

"I'm not the one who decided to get married," Alice argued. "Besides, Catherine and Charles are technically the hosts, so—"

Her voice cut away in an instant, and I turned to see what was the matter. Alice's eyes were wide and staring straight ahead. I followed her gaze to see Nicholas Whitlock walking towards us. I made a mental note to remember Nicholas Whitlock was a sure way to make Alice quiet. There was a chance I would require that particular service over the course of the week.

I stepped forward, leaving Alice blushing and frozen behind me. "Is everything all right, Mr. Whitlock?"

"Please, call me Nicholas," he insisted. Nicholas removed his derby hat and held it against his chest. "First, I would like to apologize for my grandmother's impropriety earlier."

"No, it is all right—" I started.

"It isn't," he said, shaking his head and looking up at me from beneath lowered brows. "She spends many of her days alone, and I'm afraid it makes it difficult for her to get along with others. I know I should push her to be more social, but she complains enough about travel that it is easier just to let her stay at home."

"I understand. Truly. There is no apology needed. My feelings are not so tender as to be wounded by her pointing out my obvious scar."

His mouth turned up in an attractive smile, and he shrugged. "It is not the most obvious thing about you, Miss Beckingham."

I didn't need to turn around to know Alice was glaring at me. I had no interest in Nicholas Whitlock, but even if I did, I would never pursue him at risk of breaking Alice's heart forever.

"Nicholas Whitlock." Lady Ashton mounted the stairs, threaded her arm through Alice's, and dragged the stricken girl forward to stand next to me. "It has been too long since I've seen you. Where is Aunt Augusta?"

"Inside napping," he said. "I thought I would take the opportunity to explore the grounds before she awakens."

Lady Ashton frowned. "Did she not travel with any servants?"

"She does not keep many," Nicholas said. "It is just the two of us."

"That won't do," Lady Ashton said, pursing her lips and looking around. Her eyes widened when she saw Miss Brown walking close to the wall towards the front door. She called the woman over. "Miss Brown, would you kindly attend to the needs of Miss Augusta Whitlock for the duration of her stay here at Ridgewick Hall?"

"That really won't be necessary," Nicholas started to say. "I take care of her entirely—"

"It won't be any trouble, ma'am," Miss Brown said quickly, though her eyes were trained on Nicholas, her cheeks pink. It appeared no one was immune to his many charms. "I would be happy to."

Nicholas still appeared uncertain, but Lady Ashton dismissed Miss Brown and then laid a hand on her nephew's elbow. "Everyone knows Aunt Augusta can be quite demanding. I'm sure you need a break more than you realize. Enjoy your time here and relax. And if you are going to explore the grounds, take Alice with you. She has been exploring them since she could walk."

Nicholas turned his attention to Alice, and she visibly shrunk under his gaze. "Would you mind? I wouldn't want to impose upon you."

She squeaked out an answer so quiet it was difficult to decipher, but when she crossed our small circle to stand next to Nicholas' side, sneaking quick glances up at his face, her desires became clear enough. As they walked away, Lady Ashton laughed at her daughter's crush.

"If we do not discourage her affection, Alice may change her mind about weddings yet."

6

Despite Catherine's daily insistence that everything was moments away from falling apart, the festivities carried on as planned. Additional tables and chairs were added to the back garden for the guests to enjoy, complete with fresh-cut flowers and a large white tent that took George and several of the other servants half a day to secure. The doors from the sitting room were thrown wide, allowing the guests to mill in and out of the house as they pleased, and Lady Ashton ensured the kitchen kept up a steady supply of pastries, finger foods, and tea. I even caught Aunt Augusta nodding in approval when she bit into a scone covered with clotted cream.

Miss Brown's duties quickly shifted from overseeing the household servants to overseeing solely Aunt Augusta. The poor woman was constantly running inside to fetch a fresh glass of water for the old woman or grab her a blanket. Then, when she inevitably became too warm several minutes later, the blanket had to be returned inside only to be retrieved later when a gust of wind hit her just right and gave her a chill. At meal times, Miss Brown spooned food onto Aunt Augusta's plate and cut her meat for her. Everyone watched the pair curiously, floored by the old woman's demands. Everyone except for Nicholas Whitlock.

"Are any of you gentlemen up for a bit of shooting this afternoon?" he asked with an easy smile as Miss Brown leaned across him to lift Aunt Augusta's drinking glass to her mouth.

For the first time since seeing Nicholas, Alice couldn't seem to decide whether to stare open-mouthed at him or the spectacle just to his right.

"I had no idea the woman would be so demanding," Lady Ashton said to Miss Brown as she was helping the kitchen staff clear away the plates. "I thought she would only require help climbing the stairs and getting changed for supper. I cannot decide if she simply refuses to help herself or if she is more ill than I thought."

Alice and I were still at the table even though the rest of the guests had left to retire to their rooms or walk off the meal. Nicholas was on the terrace talking with Lord Ashton and although Alice claimed she was simply too full to move, the dining room offered the most unobstructed view of the two men's conversation.

"I do not mind," Miss Brown assured my aunt. "I'm just happy to help you and Miss Catherine in any way I can."

"Maybe I can talk to her," Lady Ashton said. "I'm sure if she understood the strain she is putting on you, she wouldn't—"

"It is no strain, and I wouldn't want you to damage your relationship with family when I only need to endure for a few days."

"You are a good woman, Miss Brown."

Alice narrowed her eyes and leaned toward the doors that led to the terrace, hoping to overhear what had set Nicholas to laughing.

"You might be able to hear the conversation better if you walked out and joined it," I whispered.

She sat straight in her chair. "I'm not sure what you are talking about."

I couldn't help it. I laughed. "Alice, he is your cousin. Your handsome cousin, to be sure, but that does not change the situation."

She turned to me, eyes narrowed dangerously. "You will have to make yourself clear, cousin, because I do not understand a word you are saying."

Lady Ashton sighed. "Alice, I have enough going on in this house without having to worry about whether you'll disturb Mr. Whitlock by following him around the estate like a lost duckling."

Alice's cheeks flared a vibrant pink, and she turned towards the terrace to be sure Nicholas hadn't overheard our conversation. Meanwhile, Lady Ashton returned to encouraging Miss Brown.

"Aunt Augusta has not been seen in public for years, so I'm sure she is nervous about the ceremony and the large number of people. That does not excuse her behavior," she said, shaking her head. "But it is a possible explanation."

In the middle of Miss Brown insisting yet again that

she did not mind the task, Catherine came sprinting into the room from the kitchen, her face flushed and eyes wide.

Lady Ashton yelped in surprise and pressed a hand to her chest. "Catherine, what is it?"

"More guests." Catherine spoke as though a horde of ravenous wolves were descending upon the house.

Lady Ashton shook her head. "Everyone has already arrived. We aren't expecting more people until the picnic tomorrow."

"A car pulled into the drive just now," Catherine insisted. "The driver is removing luggage. Bags upon bags. Where ever are we going to put it all?"

"We will take care of this. I'll go sort it out right now," Lady Ashton said, laying a hand on her daughter's shoulder and hurrying out the door.

Catherine followed quickly behind. Miss Brown lingered at the table as maid servants came in and began gathering the remaining dishes from the table, and then Alice got up and left, as well. The small hunting party made up of Nicholas, Lord Ashton, and another cousin I had yet to meet were heading out to the land at the back of the estate. So, with nothing more pressing to do, I followed the women through the front doors and down the wide path to the driveway where, just as Catherine said, a car was parked.

Rolling cases and trunks were piled next to the car, and Catherine mumbled under her breath the entire walk. Just as our group reached the shallow stairs that led down to the driveway, a man slid out of the back seat of the car and then turned to assist someone. I recognized his narrow frame and sloping shoulders at once.

Lady Ashton groaned softly to herself. "Lady Harwood."

"Were we expecting her?" Catherine asked. "I don't recall inviting her."

"We had to invite her," Lady Ashton whispered. "She lives less than a mile away and has been a friend of the family for years. I just didn't believe she would actually come."

"You said the same thing about Aunt Augusta," Catherine reminded her. "And yet, she has come, too. Perhaps, we should only invite people we actually wish to attend and not hope they decide to stay home."

Lady Ashton gave her daughter a warning look, but there was no time to continue arguing as Lady Harwood and her personal physician were slowly mounting the stairs and walking towards us. Lady Harwood grunted as she made it up the last stair, wiping her forehead.

Lady Ashton held her arms wide, welcoming the pair. "Lady Harwood. Dr. Shaw. What a surprise it is to see you both here."

"I hope we have not inconvenienced you by arriving a few days early," Lady Harwood said.

"Of course, not," Lady Ashton said. Catherine's eyes went wide as she stared at her mother.

"There are no more rooms," Alice whispered to me, smiling as though she was enjoying the excitement. "Aunt Ruth and her daughters took up the last two when they arrived yesterday afternoon."

"I wanted to arrive early to allow Dr. Shaw to clean

the room to my specifications and make sure I was comfortable before the ceremony."

"The ceremony isn't for several more days," Catherine said, teeth gritted.

If Lady Harwood noticed Catherine's annoyance, she did not respond to it. "Yes, and I'm sure you have plenty to do to prepare. So, if someone could kindly show me to my room, I will stay out of everyone's way."

There was a panicked moment of silence as everyone debated how to tell Lady Harwood there was no room for her because no one had expected her to stay at the estate at all. Catherine looked to Lady Ashton, who was staring blankly forward, lost in thought. Then, all at once, she spun around, pointed at Alice, and announced that Alice would take Lady Harwood up to her room.

Alice shook her head gently. "But there is no—"

"We intended for Alice to move her things out of her room and into her cousin Rose's room before you arrived just prior to the ceremony, so you will have to give her a few minutes to make the switch now that you are here," Lady Ashton said.

Alice's mouth fell open.

"Surely, there will be fresh bedding available?" Lady Harwood asked. "After travelling, I always like to lie down for a nap."

"Yes, someone will change the bedding." Lady Ashton spun around, looking for Miss Brown, no doubt, and then turned back to Lady Harwood. "I will go inside with you and ensure everything is taken care of."

I could practically see the burdens piling on Lady Ashton's shoulders as she took Lady Harwood's arm and escorted her towards the house. Dr. Shaw followed behind, looking as weary as I'd ever seen him.

"We are sharing rooms like children now," Alice grumbled, crossing her arms over her chest much like a child would have. I wanted to point this out to her, but didn't think she would take kindly to the likeness.

"It will only be for a few days," I said, trying to comfort her. Though, I was the one who needed comforting. Alice's personality had been overbearing since the wedding planning had started in earnest, and I worried how I would feel at the end of a long week with no quiet place to rest and recover from the day.

"Catherine isn't sharing a room with anyone," she said sourly.

"That is because Catherine is the bride."

"Exactly. She should be the one who is inconvenienced." Her voice was loud enough that Dr. Shaw turned and looked over his shoulder, but when his eyes met mine, he turned back around and hastened after his employer.

The last time I'd seen the man, he'd been kneeling over the dead body of my cousin Edward. The last weekend we'd all been in this place together had been stressful, and I could see that those memories were fresh in Dr. Shaw's mind, as well.

"Is living with me going to be so horrible, Alice?" I asked, hoping to guilt Alice into complying.

She turned to me, eyes narrowed. "Don't pretend you are pleased about this, Rose. I know you'd prefer to share a room with Catherine over me."

Before I could lie and tell Alice her accusation wasn't

remotely true, she ran ahead down the walkway to stand next to her mother, probably whispering about the injustice of it all.

BEFORE THE DAY WAS THROUGH, Charles and Vivian Barry arrived at the estate, as well. When their car stopped at the top of the driveway, I thought Lady Ashton would cry.

"We are only here because we could no longer avoid the excitement," Vivian Barry said, pulling Catherine into a tight hug. "I remember romping together in the woods as children, and now you are engaged. It is such an exciting time."

"Thrilling," Catherine said, though her hands were fisted tightly at her sides.

Lady Ashton had apparently reached her breaking point and sagged, her head shaking. "I'm sorry, Charles, but we do not have any rooms available. We would love nothing more than to have you stay with us, but—"

"Oh, we have not come to stay," Charles said, his bright blond hair sparkling in the afternoon light. He turned to Catherine, nearly devouring her with his eyes. "We will return to our own home this evening. We just had to come and wish our dear friend Catherine the best of everything."

"Thank you," Catherine said curtly, avoiding his gaze.

"Funny that you are marrying another man named Charles, isn't it?" he asked.

Color rose in Catherine's neck. "It is a very common name."

"I suppose it is. Though, before her death, my mother swore the two of us would marry one day. Isn't that funny?" he asked.

"You must be a very jolly man to find so many things so funny," Catherine said with a smile that did not reach her eyes.

Lady Ashton looked between her daughter and their guest, her brow knotted quizzically, and then reached for Vivian's arm. "You two are just in time for afternoon tea. All the other guests are in the back garden. Won't you join us?"

"We would be delighted," Charles answered. "Vivian has been anxious to meet Catherine's intended. We want to make sure he is good enough for our dear Catherine."

Lady Ashton and Vivian took up the lead with Catherine and Charles Barry following behind. Catherine stayed to the far left of the pathway, doing her utmost to keep space between her and the male Barry, but Charles paid no mind to her efforts and stayed close to her side. I could not hear what they were saying, but he had his head turned towards her the entire time he spoke, staring at her face. Catherine, instead, looked straight ahead, never once meeting his eyes.

"Mr. Barry does not seem to be taking the news of Catherine's engagement well," Alice whispered, the sour mood she'd been in since learning of our new room arrangements momentarily lifted. "I believe he has come with the sole purpose of trying to stop the wedding."

"Surely not," I said as Charles pressed himself so closely to Catherine that she was forced to step off of the path and into the grass.

"He has been in love with her since they were children," Alice said.

"They've known one another that long?" I asked absently.

Alice turned to me, eyes narrowed. "You knew that, Rose. I was too young to pay much attention, but you were here during many of our weeks here when Charles would come over every day to see Catherine. He would always claim Vivian wanted to play, but everyone knew he was the one who wanted Catherine's company."

"Of course," I said quickly, waving a dismissive hand. "It slipped my mind."

Alice nodded, though I felt her gaze on me as we walked inside. Luckily, the men were returning from their hunting excursion just as we arrived inside, and Nicholas Whitlock stole her attention away.

7

Charles and Vivian left that evening after dinner just as they promised, but they returned early the next morning as breakfast was being brought out. Aunt Ruth was warm and friendly to Charles—a side of her I'd never seen before—and it quickly became apparent why.

"Margaret, tell Charles about your summer spent with the ballet," Aunt Ruth said.

Charles turned towards Ruth Blake's three daughters, searching for which one was Margaret despite the fact he had been introduced to them only the day before and reminded of their names again that morning. The three women, as they had every day since I'd made their acquaintance, were wearing similar drop-waist dresses in the same shade of green, their dark hair twisted into identical knots at the back of their thick necks.

"You were in the ballet?" Charles asked indirectly, still not sure which sister to look at.

The woman in the middle—the shortest and broadest

of the bunch—shook her head. "I assisted backstage. Lights and costumes."

"Important work," Charles said. "Without lights and costumes there would be no show."

Margaret smiled, though it looked more like a grimace, and returned to her breakfast. The sister on her right, either Ann or Helen, I couldn't be certain, perked up.

"It was an important job, which is why Margaret was relieved of her duties after she sent three of the ballerinas on stage without their skirts." She snickered.

"That was not my doing," Margaret argued, her already heavy brow lowered even further. "The dancers did not return their costumes after the previous performance."

"But it was your job to collect them," the other sister argued. "A job you failed to do that led to three dancers being half-naked on stage."

Charles' face flushed and his sister turned away from the three Blake sisters who were all beginning to turn on one another, whispering in hushed voices. "So, Charles," she said, addressing Catherine's future husband. She laughed. "It feels so strange to say that name and not be talking to my brother."

"Not that strange," Catherine mumbled. She said something else about the name being very common, though Vivian did not pay her any attention.

"We hear you are taking our Catherine back to America," she said, her lower lip pouting out. "We did hope she would return to this country. Everyone understood the desire to leave temporarily, of course. I mean, after what happened."

Her voice trailed off and the table fell into an uncomfortable silence. Lady Ashton's eyes were wide and lowered to her plate and Lord Ashton sipped his tea with a stiff upper lip and rigid posture.

"I would go anywhere in the world to be with Catherine," Charles Cresswell said, squeezing his fiancée's hand. "It just so happens she loves New York as much as I do, which works out well for me."

"New York City is so crowded," Charles Barry said, nose wrinkled. "And dirty."

"Oh, have you been?" Alice asked, turning away from watching Nicholas Whitlock eat long enough to join the conversation.

Charles licked his lips and adjusted his posture. "No, but I know many people who have been. Very few have had good things to say."

"The same could be said of London," Catherine pointed out.

Charles Barry opened his mouth to argue, but before he could, Miss Brown hurried into the room. Everyone turned towards her, and she visibly shrank under the attention and leaned down to whisper something to Lady Ashton. My aunt's face creased in concern, and she turned to her nephew.

"Nicholas, it appears your grandmother requires your assistance."

"Oh?" he asked, instantly removing his napkin from his lap and pushing away from the table. "Is she refusing to leave her room?"

Miss Brown looked around at the table as if she didn't want to have this conversation in front of everyone and then lowered her head and nodded. "Yes. She insisted that I could not be the one to bring her down. I tried to convince her, but she was becoming upset, and I—"

"I'm sure you did nothing wrong, Miss Brown," Nicholas said, his voice soft and gentle. "My grandmother can be a stubborn woman when she wants to be. I will tend to her."

He left the room and Miss Brown moved to the corner to quietly await the old woman's arrival. She looked distressed, her eyes glistening as though she was near tears, but no one paid her any attention. Lady Harwood was at the far end of the table counting out a mountain of pills handed to her by Dr. Shaw, and Aunt Ruth was trying to convince Charles Barry of the pedigree of each of her three daughters. None of the girls, however, showed any interest in Charles at all, but rather were more concerned with reminiscing about things that brought the two others some level of shame. Vivian took the opportunity brought about by Nicholas' absence to ask about his relation to the family. It was obvious immediately that she had some level of interest in him, which put Alice on guard immediately.

"He lives full-time with his grandmother," Alice said before anyone else could answer Vivian's question. "She never leaves the house, so he is holed up in her mansion all the time."

"Mansion?" Vivian asked, eyes wide with interest.

"I suppose you could call it that," Alice shrugged.

"Though, I've heard it is very run down. Barely a mansion at all."

"That isn't true," Catherine said, wrinkling her forehead at her younger sister. "Aunt Augusta is quite wealthy. She is a widow, and most people suspect Nicholas, as her favorite grandson, will inherit most of her estate."

"He truly seems to care for her," Vivian said with a smile. "It is very sweet."

"I suppose," Alice said, not sounding at all convinced. "If you want to share him with an old woman."

"Alice," Lady Ashton whispered harshly. Lady Harwood, who likely would have taken the most offense at her words, was too busy drinking water and swallowing her many pills to notice.

"Well, it is the truth," Alice said, sliding down in her seat and crossing her arms. "Until Aunt Augusta dies, Nicholas will spend much of his time caring for her. She is very ill."

Catherine took a deep breath, and I saw Charles reach across and lay a hand on his wife-to-be's leg. She smiled up at him, and I could see her physically relax. Lady Ashton turned to Lord Ashton, hoping for some assistance in wrangling their youngest daughter, but he was engrossed in the newspaper and showed no signs of having heard the current conversation at all.

Alice may have continued talking had Aunt Augusta's voice not drifted down the stairs and into the sitting room.

"I know what happened," she said, her frail voice filling the otherwise quiet house.

"It isn't that I do not believe you, Grandmother," Nicholas said softly. "It is just that there is no proof to support your accusation."

"Everyone always wants proof. As if criminal masterminds leave any proof behind," Aunt Augusta said, walking into the dining room on shaky legs, her arm wrapped around Nicholas'.

"What is this about a criminal mastermind?" Charles Barry asked, turning in his seat.

"It is nothing," Nicholas said, trying to hurry his grandmother towards her seat.

"It is not nothing," Aunt Augusta argued. She let go of her grandson's arm, and I worried for a moment she would topple over. If possible, she looked paler than she had the day before. As though the color was slowly draining out of her with each minute she was alive. She had on a thick velvet dress that covered her from neck to ankles paired with white gloves. Still, despite the warm morning air rolling through the open terrace doors, she seemed to be shivering.

"I have been robbed."

There was a quiet, collective groan from the table. Aunt Augusta had mentioned the robbery of her London home to everyone who would listen. Just yesterday, she'd told me twice, each time complaining about the lack of interest from the police and even her own grandson.

"He is a lovely boy," she'd said. "But he does not believe I was actually robbed. A person knows when they've been stolen from."

"Lord Ashton told you he would talk to the police

once we've returned to London," Lady Ashton said. "Why don't you sit and take some breakfast?"

"I'm not sure what I'm going to be able to ask them to do," Lord Ashton said.

My aunt looked at her husband and flared her nostrils in annoyance, but his attention had already returned to the newspaper.

"The London police cannot help me. We need to call the local police," she said. "Someone should send for them now."

"Grandmother," Nicholas said more sharply than I'd ever heard him speak. "Please, sit and eat something. You'll feel better."

"I will not feel better until my belongings have been returned to me." Aunt Augusta's chest was rising and falling quickly, and she was out of breath. Speaking seemed to tax her greatly, and I wondered how much Nicholas had to do for her. She seemed frailer than most. Certainly frailer than Lady Harwood, yet she'd had Dr. Shaw as her personal physician for years. I couldn't understand why Aunt Augusta wouldn't use her vast fortune to hire adequate help.

Lady Ashton stood up and moved to Aunt Augusta's other side, trying to urge her forward. The old woman remained resolute. "There is nothing we can do about what was stolen from you now. I know it is upsetting, but you should really try to forget about it until you are back in London."

"I cannot wait until I'm back in London," she said, tongue darting out to wet her thin lips. "This matter must be resolved now, while the thief is still here among us."

At this, the entire table, which had moments before been doing their best to ignore Aunt Augusta's outburst, turned. Aunt Ruth leaned around Charles Barry. "What do you mean the thief is among us?"

"Certainly you are not suggesting one of us stole from you?" Vivian Barry asked, a superior smile on her face.

"We've all heard of your vast wealth, Mrs. Whitlock," Charles Barry said, leaning forward with an expression identical to his sister's spread across his face. "But no one in this room is bad enough off to stoop to stealing." He stopped and turned to the other Charles. "At least, as far as I am aware."

Catherine glared at the male Barry, but Charles Cresswell laid a comforting hand on his fiancée's elbow and did not respond. Charles Barry, unable to get a rise out of his target, turned back to Aunt Augusta.

"I would never insult your guests," Aunt Augusta said to Lady Ashton, who bowed her head in gratitude. "Your staff, however, I cannot speak as highly of."

Lady Ashton's gratitude turned to suspicion. "Are you accusing my servants of stealing from you? Because I can assure you they have all worked for me for years without incident. I will vouch for every single one of them."

"Please, Grandmother," Nicholas said, his cheeks growing red. "Let's not do this now."

"It must be done now," Aunt Augusta said, stepping backwards, momentarily losing her balance and having to catch herself on the door frame. She slowly turned away from the table to look directly at Miss Brown.

Lady Ashton's personal attendant had been silent throughout the entire ordeal, and she remained still enough that I almost forgot she was in the room at all. However, as soon as Aunt Augusta turned her attention to her, Miss Brown seemed to glow from head to toe. Her brown eyes widened until a circle of white haloed around her irises. She looked to Lady Ashton and then to the rest of the table as though looking for someone to help her, but everyone at the table was as stricken as she was, unsure what to do.

"This woman took advantage of me," Aunt Augusta said, lifting a trembling arm to point at Miss Brown. "She thought I was too old to notice when my things go missing. She thought I wouldn't be aware enough to catch her in the act, but I have done it, and I will not rest until she has been brought to justice."

Lady Ashton's mouth was hanging open. She turned to her husband for help, and finally, Lord Ashton had lowered his paper, but he did not seem particularly ready to take any action. Lady Ashton laid a hand on Aunt Augusta's shoulder.

"Aunt Augusta, I do not at all want to diminish your claim, but Miss Brown has been in my home for the better part of a year. She has always been a helpful, willing employee, and I have every faith in her."

Miss Brown sagged with relief, but her back went rigid again when Aunt Augusta pulled away from Lady Ashton and took a step towards her.

"I cannot say whether this woman has served you well or not," she said, pausing to cough, her chest rattling violently. "I can only speak to her performance while assisting me. I arrived yesterday with a small box of jewelry that is important to me. Important enough that I did not want to leave it behind in London in case the thieves who robbed me before should return. This morning, however, when I opened the box, a cherished necklace was missing. I searched my room, but there was no trace of it. And the last person to have opened the box was your Miss Brown when she replaced my earrings there last night before I retired for the evening."

"Perhaps, you did not bring it with you," Nicholas said. "Which necklace was it? It may very well be in your bedroom in London."

Aunt Augusta shook her head. "It was the necklace given to me by my mother the day of my wedding. It is not an item I would misplace or forget."

Nicholas bit his lower lip, and I could tell he knew the necklace at once. Lady Ashton looked to him, hoping he would continue trying to calm his grandmother, but it appeared he was giving up. My aunt looked helplessly once more to her husband before turning back to her guests, her eyes eventually landing on me. I could see the plea in her eyes, so with no idea what I would do, I stepped away from the table and crossed the room.

"I'm sure this can be settled," I said.

"It will be settled when my property is returned to me," the old woman said, eyes narrowed at me. "And I would appreciate it if you would keep out of it. This is a family matter."

"Rose is family," Lady Ashton said sternly, moving to lay an arm around my shoulder.

There was enough going on that Lady Ashton did not need to worry about defending me, as well, but I appreciated it nonetheless.

"Regardless," Aunt Augusta said only slightly less haughty. "The matter will not be resolved happily until my necklace is returned."

Finally, Miss Brown stepped forward, and Lady Ashton gestured for her to speak. "Yes, Miss Brown. Please come forward and tell us your side of the story."

"There is little to tell," Miss Brown said softly, refusing to look Aunt Augusta in the eyes. "I did not steal anything. I would never take something that did not belong to me."

Aunt Augusta huffed, and Nicholas frowned at his grandmother, though his admonition did little to stifle her anger.

"I stayed close to her like you asked me to, Lady Ashton, but I only opened her jewelry box to place her earrings in it as she already stated. Beyond that, I did not go near it." She finished her statement with a small bow and stepped back into the shadows around the edges of the room.

Lady Ashton smiled kindly at the woman, and then turned to Aunt Augusta. "I have no reason to suspect Miss Brown would steal from you, Aunt Augusta, so I have to believe her until I have reason to think otherwise. I am happy to assist you in searching for the necklace, but beyond that, there is nothing I can do."

"Start searching in her quarters," Aunt Augusta shouted—as much as her weak lungs would allow, anyway. She pointed a crooked finger at the woman. "I'm sure we will find it straightaway."

Lady Ashton began to shake her head, but Miss

Brown interrupted before she could say anything. "I shall gladly allow it if it will clear my name."

"Miss Brown," Lady Ashton said, frowning. "I do not want to disrespect you in that way—"

"Do it and be done with it," Lord Ashton said. He had not even bothered to look up from his paper, but he waved a hand over the top and continued. "If we find the necklace, she will be dismissed at once. If we do not, then the matter will be put to rest, and we will not discuss it again."

The color drained from Miss Brown's face at the suggestion of her dismissal, but she nodded. "That sounds fair to me."

Aunt Augusta's top lip curled back. "Fine, but it must be done immediately. Before she has a chance to hide the necklace."

Lady Ashton looked longingly towards the breakfast table for a moment. She deserved a long rest more than anyone in the house. Every moment had been filled with entertaining guests and keeping Catherine from dissolving into a puddle of worry. Yet, another crisis called.

Lady Ashton led Miss Brown towards the hallway where the servant's quarters were located. Just before they left the room, she turned and gestured for me to follow, as well.

"Would you mind assisting in the search, Rose? You have a keen eye for this kind of thing."

I wanted nothing more than to remain out of the matter altogether, but I would not refuse my aunt anything when she had so much to worry about. I followed Nicholas and his grandmother down the hall, and when I heard footsteps behind me, turned to see Alice in my wake. I wanted to tell her to go back to the dining room, but knew it would do no good.

Miss Brown's room was small and tidy. Her bed was made, the blankets tucked under the corners, and she had three identical dresses hanging in a small closet with an extra pair of thick-heeled shoes sitting neatly on the floor. There was no chest of drawers or trunks to search. Just a wooden table with a lamp and a Bible next to the bed and the closet. Everyone stood outside the room in the hallway while I stepped inside and spun in a circle twice.

"Search," Aunt Augusta urged. She turned to Lady Ashton. "What is she waiting for?"

"There is nowhere to hide anything in here," I said. "Unless you want to tear up the floorboards."

"Perhaps, it is on her person," Aunt Augusta said, turning slowly to Miss Brown, milky eyes narrowed. She was leaning especially heavily on Nicholas now. It would not be long before she'd need to take a seat and rest. She'd just woken up, but already the day had been a busy one.

"I will not have her searched like a criminal when there is no proof she did anything wrong," Lady Ashton said. She stepped into the small room herself and then moved towards the closet. She slid each dress one at a time towards the right side of the closet.

"There," Aunt Augusta said, pointing to the closet. "That is my dress hanging in her closet."

Nicholas Whitlock moved forward at once, stepping

into the room and offering to search in Lady Ashton's place. He pulled a long, dark velvet gown identical to the one Augusta had on from the back of Miss Brown's closet. "This gown?"

"I was going to clean it for her," Miss Brown said in her defense. "There was a mud stain on the hem from her walk yesterday, and I brought it down to brush it away. I was going to return it to her closet this afternoon."

"That is a reasonable explanation." Nicholas laid the dress over his arm and turned to his grandmother. She scowled and instructed him to continue searching.

Nicholas sighed, shrugged his shoulders at me in apology, and began to search. Or, search as much as possible in the small space. Lady Ashton returned to the closet, running her hands uselessly along the walls, and I flipped through the pages of Miss Brown's Bible. Many passages were underlined, and she had written copious notes in the margins. Once I finished with the Bible, I circled a finger around the inside of the lampshade and then bent down to check on the underside of the table, as well. There was nothing.

Nicholas was checking the bed, following his grandmother's instructions as she asked him to remove Miss Brown's pillow case, massage the pillow to see if she had sewn the necklace inside the stuffing, and look underneath the mattress.

"Aunt Augusta," Lady Ashton said when the old woman suggested we cut open the mattress. "I do not believe we are going to find anything here. The room is spotless. If it was here, we would have found it—"

"Oh dear."

Lady Ashton went quiet, and everyone in the room and waiting in the hallway went silent, as well. We turned to watch as Nicholas Whitlock grabbed something from under the mattress and stood up. His hand uncurled slightly, and a gold chain fell out of his grip. And hanging from the chain was a golden oval-shaped locket.

"That is mine," Aunt Augusta said at once, her voice breaking the quiet.

I could see Miss Brown standing behind her, face drained of color, eyes wide in shock. She said nothing, but shook her head.

"No," Lady Ashton said, in obvious dismay. "Surely not."

"It is." Augusta stepped forward on shaky legs, gripping the door frame as she reached out and took the necklace from Nicholas. "This is my mother's necklace."

She held it into the air, and I got a better look at it. The gold was tarnished, and there was a setting in the center of the locket where a gem was once set, but it was now empty. The necklace was worthless. The only value it held was sentimental, and yet, Miss Brown had taken it. Why?

Lady Ashton asked the same question. "Why, Miss Brown?"

There were tears in the young woman's eyes now. Her timidity began to fade as desperation took over. She pushed through the crowd of onlookers, shoving aside Alice, who was watching the proceedings with hungry eyes. "I didn't take it. I wouldn't. I have no idea how it ended up there."

"Liar," Aunt Augusta said, tucking the necklace into

her pocket. "I will leave you to pack your things. Lady Ashton, you may want to check the rest of her belongings and make sure she is not leaving with any of your precious valuables."

Miss Brown let out a sob as Aunt Augusta and a sober looking Nicholas left the room together. Alice was still clinging to the doorframe, enthralled and horrified.

"I swear I didn't take it," Miss Brown said, clutching at Lady Ashton's hands. "You must believe me."

I could see in my aunt's face that she was weary and wanted nothing more than to trust the woman who had done her utmost to make her life easier over the last few months. Miss Brown had assisted the family through some of their darkest days, and Lady Ashton had come to view Miss Brown as more than an employee. However, I could also see that she was torn.

"Lady Ashton?" Miss Brown asked, her voice breaking.

My aunt shook her head. "I...I'm not sure what I am supposed to do."

Miss Brown dropped her employer's hands and stepped away, something in her eyes hardening.

"You must let her go." Catherine was standing in the door now, her eyes downturned and sorrowful. "It is the deal father made with Aunt Augusta. She is in the dining room informing all of the other guests."

"But I do not know if she did it," Lady Ashton said.

"I didn't," Miss Brown insisted, fisting her hands at her sides.

"It does not matter," Catherine said. "If we do not let

her go, the other guests will never rest easy. It will be a cloud over the entire wedding ceremony."

"Not everything is about your ceremony," Alice argued from the doorway.

Catherine snapped around to frown at her sister before moving forward to stand by her mother. "I know Miss Brown has been a friend to you, but she has put us in a bad position. We do not have many options."

"We can send Aunt Augusta away," Alice whispered.

Catherine turned on her sister. "That would mean Nicholas Whitlock would leave, as well."

Alice's cheeks flushed, but the threat hit its mark. Alice pinched her lips together.

"If Miss Brown stays, there will be no way to salvage the rest of the week," Catherine said. "Even if Aunt Augusta becomes angry enough to leave, the rest of the guests will doubt our judgment and our help."

I saw the moment Lady Ashton accepted the truth. Her shoulders shrugged forward, and she looked up at Miss Brown from beneath lowered lashes. "I'm sorry, Miss Brown. You will have to pack your things. George can give you a ride into town."

Miss Brown staggered back as though she'd been slapped. Her expression changed from disbelief to sadness to anger in an instant. "But I did nothing wrong."

Lady Ashton's mouth opened and closed several times before she finally spoke. "There is no other option."

"Yes, there is. Do not dismiss me on the word of a horrid old woman when I did nothing wrong." Her voice was loud enough that everyone in the dining room could hear her, and Aunt Augusta could be heard gasping in offense.

Lady Ashton frowned and lowered her head. "I'm sorry, Miss Brown. Please pack your things."

"I won't." Miss Brown stumbled backwards through the door and into the hallway, her face growing red. "I do not deserve this, and I will not allow my good name to be soiled because of a suspicious, vindictive old woman."

"Watch the way you speak about me," Lady Augusta called from the dining room.

"Be quiet," Miss Brown hollered. "You've done more than enough already, but if I have anything to say about it, this will be the last time you treat anyone this way."

Aunt Augusta muttered something to Nicholas about stopping the woman from speaking so about her, but it did not matter. Before Lady Ashton could calm her or Nicholas could step forward to defend his grandmother's name, Miss Brown ran down the hallway and exited through a servant's door in the back of the house. When Alice ran after her a few moments later, there was no sign of her in the garden or the tree line. Miss Brown was gone.

8

Catherine and Lady Ashton did their best to keep the guests from discussing the situation between Miss Brown and Aunt Augusta in too much length, but it was hopeless. The excitement from breakfast lasted well into the evening. Even Nicholas Whitlock could not hold his tongue once he'd had a few after dinner drinks.

"Imagine stealing from an old woman," he'd said, shaking his head. "It is a horrible thing to do, though the crime itself leads me to believe this was her first offense."

"Why do you say so?" Lord Ashton asked.

"Because she stole jewelry." He took another drink and then wrinkled his nose. "You should never steal jewelry. It is too easy to identify. You want to steal money. No one marks their money. Once you take it from their coin purse, the victim cannot prove whether it is theirs or whether you've had it all along."

"Maybe she meant to sell the necklace," Charles Barry suggested.

"Perhaps," Nicholas said.

"According to Catherine, the necklace was not even very nice and wouldn't have been worth much," Charles Cresswell said. "And Catherine would know. She has very fine tastes."

Mr. Barry pulled back his top lip in distaste at the mention of Catherine.

"Another proof that she is not a skilled thief," Nicholas said.

Catherine retired early to avoid the constant talk of the event that had officially overshadowed her wedding, whereas when I went to bed, I had to listen to Alice discuss the altercation until she became too exhausted to keep her eyes open.

If Catherine hoped to awaken with the news from the day before forgotten, she was disappointed. Even with the back garden transformed into a lavish tea party complete with freshly-cut flowers filling the vases I'd purchased in London, trays of desserts and pastries on every table, and every guest dressed in their best, no one could help but whisper about the drama in small groups as Aunt Augusta moved slowly among the crowd, the worthless locket hanging from her neck like a prize.

The drama the day before seemed to have left her exhausted. Her skin, which had been pale and papery, seemed to have taken on a gray and clammy sheen. As early morning turned to midday and the sun rose in the sky, she actually removed her jacket and bared her arms, which were crisscrossed with blue veins and purple bruises.

Vivian Barry expressed her concern for the old

woman by laying her hand on Nicholas Whitlock's arm. "Your poor grandmother does not look well. I do not think the heat is agreeing with her."

"I've tried to send her inside several times already," he said with a shrug, adjusting his top hat over his dark hair. "She refuses to take orders from anyone, including me. There is nothing to be done."

"You are a very adoring grandson," Vivian said with a smile, eyelashes fluttering. When Nicholas turned away from her to watch his grandmother limp across the garden, she quickly rearranged her bright blonde hair beneath her lace headband, pulling a strand down across her forehead. "Not many men would be willing to care for an elderly woman the way you do."

"Then you do not know the right kind of men, sister," Charles Barry said loudly, his gaze slipping over to where Catherine and Charles were entertaining Aunt Ruth and her three daughters. "I would be happy to care for an ailing family member if we had any."

Vivian frowned at her brother and pulled closer to Nicholas, which finally spurred Alice to step forward and engage the female Barry in conversation.

"You and your brother are so close, Vivian," she said, a bright, genuine smile spread across her face. "Many people have to be informed that you two are not husband and wife. Did you realize that, Nicholas?"

Vivian's cheeks flamed red, but her smile never faltered.

"Realize what?" Nicholas asked, tearing his eyes from where Aunt Augusta was teetering on the edge of the fish pond, looking like she could tumble in from a stiff wind at any moment.

"That Charles and Vivian are siblings and not a married couple," Alice repeated just as cheerfully as the first time. "Many people make that mistake because they are so unusually close."

"We are closer that most," Vivian said. "Though, I do not count it unusual. Perhaps, your perception is skewed because of your own relationship with your brother."

I watched as a violent glint appeared in Alice's eyes, and decided it would be pointless to try and sway Alice to be civil, so instead I removed the source of the women's struggle.

"Nicholas, I have had my eye on the dessert table for awhile and can no longer resist. Would you care to sample a few things with me?"

Nicholas offered me his elbow without hesitation, and we left Vivian and Alice behind, glaring at one another. As we walked, Nicholas did not talk to me, but rather kept his attention on his grandmother.

"Are you worried for her?" I asked finally.

Nicholas startled as though surprised by my presence and then laughed at himself. "Sorry. I am being quite rude."

"No need to apologize."

He looked down at me, blue eyes bright and clear. "My grandmother doesn't leave the house often, and I am nervous about how she is doing."

I nodded. "I understand. Though, if you want my opinion, she seemed in perfect health yesterday morning."

He ran a hand across his cheek and shook his head. "In the end, she was right about Miss Brown, but I still wish the whole mess had never happened. The poor woman lost her job because of a broken locket. It hardly seems fair."

"Yes," I agreed. "But she did steal. That is not something that can be tolerated."

"No, but I would have liked to pull her aside privately and announce the news rather than embarrass her in front of a house of guests."

"Yes, that was unfortunate." I had never seen Miss Brown be anything but kind and accommodating, but the image of her, red-faced and running from Ridgewick Hall would not leave me any time soon.

We reached the dessert table, and I placed a sampling of small treats on my plate. Nicholas did the same, though he made no move to eat them.

"I hope our coming to the wedding has not caused more trouble that it was worth," he said, staring over as his grandmother walked from the pond back towards the party, her head lowered. "I'm sorry to admit she is not as friendly to the outside world as she is to me. Most people do not appreciate her the way I do."

I couldn't imagine anyone appreciating Aunt Augusta's company, but I did not admit that to Nicholas. "Perhaps, that is why she likes you, then. You appreciate her, therefore, she appreciates you."

"Perhaps." He smiled.

Just then, Aunt Augusta stumbled in the grass. I wouldn't have noticed at all except that when she did,

Lady Harwood let out a shriek, alerting the entire gathering to the matter.

"Dr. Shaw," she yelled. "Help Mrs. Whitlock. Hurry."

Aunt Ruth grabbed her three daughters and yanked them out of the way as though a car was rushing towards them as Dr. Shaw dropped his plate of dessert and hurried past them and a table where Catherine and Charles Cresswell were entertaining a group of local gentry. As soon as he reached Aunt Augusta, who had managed to right herself and shuffle forward to an empty table, he grabbed her elbow.

"Do not touch me," the old woman screamed, her voice hoarse and raw. Dark circles were gathering under her eyes, and I could tell even from across the party that her hands were the pale white of fresh snow. "I am capable of caring for myself."

Lady Harwood grabbed her cane, having left her usual wheelchair inside the house, and took several steps towards where Dr. Shaw was backing away from Aunt Augusta, his hands in the air. "There is no shame in asking for help, my dear woman."

"I am not your 'dear' anything," Augusta claimed. "The only person here I care about remotely is my grandson, and he is the one who helps me. I do not need you or your doctor."

Lady Harwood's lips pursed, and she placed a hand to her chest. "I have never been treated so for offering someone assistance. I am only keeping an eye on you because your grandson seems more interested in the young women at this party than with your wellbeing."

Nicholas laid his plate on the table, nodded his head

to me in apology, and crossed the grass to assist his grandmother. When he reached her, he ran a soothing hand along her back and then pressed the back of his hand to her forehead. He whispered something to her I could not hear, and she smiled up at him. She truly did like him better than anyone else.

"Mr. Whitlock did nothing to deserve this unkindness," Vivian Barry said, stepping forward to defend him since he showed no signs of defending himself.

"He did not," Lady Harwood agreed. "Which is why it is not an unkindness. It is the truth. Mrs. Whitlock should consider hiring professional help before her grandson leaves her to flirt with half the country.

"Lady Harwood," Charles Cresswell said. "I know you are upset, but please let's try and stay calm."

Suddenly, Charles Barry entered the scene, as well, stepping in front of Charles Cresswell to speak with Lady Harwood. "There is no need to attack any of the other guests. You did your duty by offering help to a woman in need, and it is no fault of yours if she is too stubborn to accept it."

"Watch your words," Nicholas warned, finally offering some kind of defense. "My grandmother does not owe anyone here an explanation for her actions. Especially you."

"Especially me?" Charles Barry asked, chin tucked in, eyes narrowed. "What does that mean?"

"It means she could buy your home and ten homes around it without hesitation," Nicholas said.

Mr. Barry's eyes narrowed, but before he could say anything, Charles Cresswell stepped between the two men. "I am sorry, gentleman, but I cannot allow you to hash out this fight here. My fiancée is distressed enough as it is. Please do not add to it."

"I would never do anything to upset Catherine," Charles Barry said, straightening his bow tie and stepping away with one last glare in Nicholas Whitlock's direction.

Charles walked back towards where his sister was standing stonily with Alice, but as he reached her, she rushed past him to get to Nicholas and his grandmother. She said something to Aunt Augusta, but the words were drowned out in a loud, violent coughing fit. Nicholas patted his grandmother's back gently, massaging soothing circles across her back and shoulders. Vivian hurried away to fetch the old woman a drink of water.

"She is acting like a servant to impress him," Alice whispered to me. I hadn't realized she'd walked over to stand next to me, so I jumped as she spoke. She laughed. "Everyone is very on edge. Catherine looks like she might scream at any moment."

I wished I could be as calm as Alice was. She seemed to treat everyone and everything—save for Nicholas Whitlock—at the wedding as a joke. She showed no concern for her sister's wedding ceremony or her mother's wellbeing as Lady Ashton hurried back and forth between Lady Harwood and Aunt Augusta to see if either of the old women needed anything. The stress of the last several days and nonstop company in the form of Alice had finally begun to take its toll on me.

"At least Vivian Barry is trying to help," I said sharply. "It is better to be a servant than a spoiled daughter of wealthy parents who does nothing other than relentlessly tease those around her."

As soon as the words were out of my mouth, I knew they were unforgivable by Alice's standards, but it was too late. Her pink lips puckered into an angry knot, and before I could apologize or explain, she stomped away in the direction of the house.

As if things were not in chaos enough, just as Alice stomped into the house, the doors to the kitchen opened and the head chef came through the doors with a two-layer fruit cake in his hands. "Congratulations to the happy couple."

Charles Cresswell hurried over to stand next to Catherine as the cake was placed in the center of the table, and the rest of the guests—including a fuming Lady Harwood and her humble physician, Vivian Barry who tried and failed to escort Aunt Augusta forward, and Charles Barry with a noticeably overflowing glass of wine —stepped forward, clapping and doing their best to pretend they cared about the upcoming wedding in any way.

Lord Ashton didn't even do that much. He was standing over by the pond where Aunt Augusta had been a few minutes before, staring down into the water like he wanted to jump in. Lady Ashton hurried over to pull him into the party, but he shrugged away her efforts. When my aunt turned around and met my eyes, I tried to quickly focus my attention on the cake, so she would not know I had seen, but I knew I'd been caught. For days, I and everyone else had tried to convince Catherine that everything was going well. That her wedding would not be a failure and it would go off without a hitch. However, just in the small group of people in front of me, I spotted several hitches. It didn't appear as though things could get worse.

Once the cake was sliced and handed out, the guests were busy enough eating that no one was fighting, and I thought it would be a good time to go inside and try to find Alice. She had been such a help to me over the last few days, ensuring I didn't make a fool of myself in front of family members and old friends I could not remember, and I'd rewarded her by insulting her character. Even if Alice was in need of some reprimanding, it should not have come from me, and it was only right that I should go apologize. So, I refused a slice of cake from a servant and smoothed my sweaty hands down the beaded tulle of my dress. It was midday and already hot enough that I was uncomfortable. I could not begin to imagine how Aunt Augusta was enduring it in her usual velvet gown.

Just as the old woman crossed my mind, I heard a scream from the garden behind me. When I turned around, the guests were descending towards a table in the center. Lady Harwood was screaming for Dr. Shaw and Lady Ashton was waving her arms, trying to keep everyone away. I could not see Catherine or Charles, though I could see Vivian and Charles Barry standing off to the side, twin expressions of horror on their faces.

As I got closer, quickening my pace to figure out what had happened, Aunt Ruth and her three daughters moved to the right, and I saw a pale, blue-veined leg lying in the grass.

"Grandmother!" Nicholas Whitlock's voice rose over

the commotion. I moved around Aunt Ruth and saw him kneeling in the grass, his hand on the back of his grandmother's neck, trying to lift her up. "Grandmother, can you hear me?"

Dr. Shaw was on the other side of Aunt Augusta, running his fingers under the sleeve of her gown to feel at her pulse. He probed in several different locations, pausing each time and staring up at the sky. Finally, he lowered his hand and shook his head.

"What happened?" I asked, trying to understand how everything could have fallen apart when I'd only been gone for half a minute.

Dr. Shaw stood up and brushed mud from the knees of his pants. He looked at me and then scanned the rest of the guests. "Augusta Whitlock is dead."

9

"This is my fault. I killed her," Nicholas said again, his face buried in his hands.

Charles Cresswell patted the grieving man's back. "You didn't do anything wrong, Nicholas. It was an accident."

Nicholas lifted his head and shook it, his lips pinched together, trying not to cry. Then, suddenly, he struck out, his fist slamming onto the table. "I should have been taking better care of her. It was my duty to watch her, and I didn't do it. If I had stayed closer to her, I may have noticed her growing more ill."

I set down a cup of tea in front of him, pushing it towards him. He needed to eat or drink something. It had been hours since the party, and he hadn't done anything other than blame himself.

"We all saw her, Nicholas. No one noticed her acting unusual," I said. Though, this wasn't entirely true. I had noticed her color changing dramatically throughout the last few days, and everyone had seen her stumble and become dizzy. Though, I, like everyone else, associated this with her normal behavior. She was an old woman. Failing health was expected at a certain age.

He pushed the tea away and stood up, pacing across the sitting room. "I should have noticed. It was my duty to notice. She asked me to care for her, and I allowed myself to be distracted. I allowed her to be cared for by a thief." Suddenly, he raised a finger in the air, eyes wide. "The stress of that confrontation probably played a part in her downfall. She slept all afternoon after Miss Brown was dismissed."

Miss Brown had already been accused of theft, so it seemed wrong to also pin Aunt Augusta's death on her. Besides, Aunt Augusta seemed to live her life in constant confrontation. I doubted whether one argument with a servant could have played any role in her demise, however Nicholas was not in a place to hear reason, so I decided to simply listen.

"I cannot believe this," Catherine said, sipping on her fourth cup of tea. She grabbed her fiancé's hand and pulled him closer to her, twining her fingers through his. "What are the chances?"

I knew what she meant. Another death at Ridgewick. The death of Mr. Matcham had been weighing heavily on the minds of those who had been at the last gathering at Ridgewick Hall, but no one thought it could possibly happen again. Yet, here we were, once again waiting inside while the police collected a body.

Suddenly, the door to the terrace opened, and everyone turned as Dr. Shaw, Lady Ashton, and Lord Ashton walked inside.

"How did she die?" Lady Harwood and Alice asked at the same time.

Alice had not spoken to me once since the party. It seemed even the death of a wedding guest was not enough of a distraction for her to forgive me for what I'd said.

"Is it contagious?" Lady Harwood asked, rubbing her hands together as though she was washing them.

Nicholas looked up at the trio in clear agony. His handsome features were twisted in grief.

"No one has any reason to worry," Lady Ashton said, collapsing into an open seat at the end of the sofa. "Aunt Augusta died of natural causes."

"Is that true?" Lady Harwood asked her personal physician, not trusting Lady Ashton's assessment.

Dr. Shaw had his black medical bag at his side—the same bag I'd once searched for signs of a poison vial. He lowered it to the ground and ran the back of his hand across his forehead, clearing away a sheen of sweat. "It is true. The poor woman was old and in ill-health. There is no reason to think her death was caused by anything other than a failing body."

Lady Harwood sighed with relief, but Nicholas Whitlock sagged in his chair and lowered his head into his lap. His shoulders shook with sobs.

Vivian Barry stepped forward to comfort him, but before she could reach him, Alice slid into place at his side, laying an arm over his shoulders. Vivian wrinkled her brow, but stepped away. Despite all of the horrible circumstances, I found myself smiling at Alice's determination. I had to bite back the smile to keep from looking inconsiderate.

"So, natural causes?" Charles Barry asked from the back of the room. Since Augusta's death, he had taken to drinking even more, and his voice was now slurred. "We do not need to worry about a plague?"

Lady Harwood gasped and began rubbing her hands together nervously again, as though just the mention of the word 'plague' would bring one into being.

"Natural causes," Dr. Shaw reiterated.

As he said the words, the memory of him making a similar announcement came back to me. It had been in regards to the death of Mr. Matcham. His death was also believed to have been natural. Until I proved otherwise.

However, Aunt Augusta was not Mr. Matcham, I reminded myself. She was an elderly woman in ill-health. It was not unusual for elderly women in ill-health to die suddenly. Though, a point could be made that women who came from such wealth did not die so suddenly. They were attended to by nurses and physicians. They died quietly in their beds, surrounded by loved ones. Not in the middle of a tea party after fighting with the guests.

Nicholas' sobs pulled me from my thoughts, and I realized something else unusual. Nicholas had inherited a good deal of his grandmother's wealth. Within just a few hours, Nicholas Whitlock had become the wealthiest person in the room.

10

Aunt Augusta's body had been removed from the grass and taken back to the police station, but everyone seemed keen to avoid the back garden, anyway. Guests sat on the front porch or paced along the path in front of Ridgewick Hall, but most of them remained indoors entirely. The house, which the day before had been filled with talk and laughter, felt eerily silent.

"This death is going to cast a shadow over the entire event," Catherine said.

Lord and Lady Ashton, Catherine and Charles, and Alice and I had all gathered in one of the sitting rooms. As soon as I arrived, Lady Ashton asked a servant to pull the doors shut and leave so we could discuss matters. I didn't know what there was to discuss until I saw Catherine's face, her red, puffy eyes and damp cheeks.

"Everything is ruined," she said, squeezing Charles' hand until I thought he would cry out in pain. "This was supposed to be a celebration, and now it is a wake."

"It is not a wake," Lady Ashton insisted. "Most of our guests didn't even know Aunt Augusta. And those who did didn't know her well enough to mourn. Nicholas Whitlock is the only exception."

Catherine snorted through a sob. "The most important exception. He hasn't stopped crying for hours."

"The wound is fresh," Alice said, defending him. "He lost someone very close to him."

Catherine wiped her hands across her cheeks and sniffled, sitting tall. She had never been an overly emotional woman, but it seemed the stress of the last few days had finally become overwhelming. I could not blame her.

"I understand that," Catherine said. "But that does not mean I want his time of mourning to interfere with my wedding day."

"There are more important things than your wedding, *Catherine*." Alice said her sister's name like an insult.

"Girls," Lady Ashton warned before the argument could escalate. She turned briefly to Lord Ashton, but he was staring out the window, seemingly lost in thought. She sighed and looked back to her daughters. "Emotions are high right now, but I truly believe things will calm down and the wedding will carry on unscathed."

"How?" Catherine asked. "A woman died."

"A woman no one cared for to begin with," Alice said, momentarily switching sides to comfort her sister.

Lady Ashton frowned and shook her head at Alice, though she did not disagree with her. It was hard to deny the truth of her statement. Aunt Augusta had made little effort to socialize or be friendly towards the other wedding guests. Even her own family knew very little about her beyond the fact that she was a wealthy shut-in who often accused others of thievery.

"That may be true, but there are other problems beyond the death," Catherine said.

"Such as?" Lady Ashton asked.

Catherine twisted her lips to the side in thought and then pointed to her fiancé. "Charles Barry will not stop trying to insult Charles. I have not spoken to him in almost a year, but he acts like he is moments away from calling a duel for my honor."

"I am not concerned about Mr. Barry," Charles said, smoothing a hand down Catherine's arm. "Do not worry yourself about him on my account."

"What of Vivian?" Alice offered, drawing a warning glare from Lady Ashton. The last thing Catherine needed was more problems to worry about. "She has been throwing herself at Nicholas Whitlock at every opportunity. At this rate, our guests may wonder whether we've invited a lady of the night."

Lady Ashton gasped. "Alice Beckingham."

"That is cruel, Alice," Catherine said, shaking her head.

Alice shrugged and my aunt closed her eyes and sighed. "We just need to remain positive. Though Augusta's death was unforeseen, it has done nothing to upset our schedule or our planning. We can still move forward with the wedding, and isn't that the most important thing?"

"Yes," Alice agreed. "Plus, now that Aunt Augusta

does not need her room, Rose and I will not have to share."

She didn't look at me as she spoke, though it felt like a small victory that she even said my name.

"You are going to stay in the dead woman's room, Alice?" Catherine asked, eyebrow raised.

Alice's eyes went wide, but before she could say anything, I cleared my throat. "I am happy to move into her room, Alice. You may have my room."

My youngest cousin still would not look at me, but I saw her shoulders relax slightly.

"That is very kind of you, Rose," Lady Ashton said, smiling gratefully. Then, she turned back to the room. "See? Everything is going just fine."

As she spoke, there was a knock at the sitting room doors. Then, the doors pushed open and Aunt Ruth stepped inside, hands folded behind her back. "Do you all have a moment?"

"Of course," Lord Ashton said. "You are family."

Aunt Ruth stepped inside, and as she did, her three daughters followed in behind her, eyes wide and searching. They each wore travel skirts in the same shade of brown with matching sweaters that had a striped pattern similar to the wallpaper. I'd been around the three women for the better part of a week, and I was no closer to being able to remember who was who.

"We are grateful for your hospitality," Aunt Ruth began, hands folded behind her back. She shifted forward onto the toes of her shoes and then back to her heels. "But we will be relocating to the Inn in the village for the remainder of our visit."

Lady Ashton frowned and turned to her husband. Lord Ashton pressed his lips together firmly. "I can assure you, sister, there is no need for that. You are safe within these walls."

For the first time since I'd met her, Aunt Ruth smiled. The simple act seemed to require a great deal of energy. Her lips trembled, and her breathing became more noticeable, her chest rising and falling quickly. "I never doubted that for a moment. I feel very safe here. As do my girls."

"Then why do you feel the need to leave?" Lady Ashton asked, her voice sharper than usual.

Aunt Ruth rubbed her lips together. Behind her, Margaret, Ann, and Helen, were gazing up at the ceiling, the floor, and their own hands—looking anywhere but straight ahead at where we were sitting in front of them. "The four of us take up two of your rooms, and I know you have more guests than you originally planned for. Since we will be just as happy at the Inn, we thought we would stay there until the wedding to free up more room for your other guests."

"Actually, we have fewer guests than we originally planned for," Lady Ashton said, referencing the now empty room that had been occupied by Augusta Whitlock until that morning. "There is no need to spend the money and pack up your belongings."

"We are already packed," Aunt Ruth said. "In fact, we are leaving now."

"Now?" Lady Ashton looked to her husband for help, but he was no longer taking part in the conversation. His gaze had returned to the window.

"Yes. Our belongings are being loaded into a car as we speak." Aunt Ruth stepped backwards, bumping into one of her daughters—perhaps Margaret, though I couldn't be certain. The girls giggled and shuffled into a line, heading for the door.

"Are you certain?" Lady Ashton asked.

Alice mumbled something under her breath that sounded like "Let them leave," and Catherine nudged her sister in the arm, quieting her with lowered brows.

"Positive," Aunt Ruth said, pushing her daughters through the door into the entrance hall. "We will see you all at the wedding."

Before anyone could argue further, the Blake women were gone. Moments later, the front door slammed shut behind them. I turned just in time to see them rushing down the front path to the waiting car. One of the women turned back to get one last look at the house over her shoulder, and I would have sworn I saw fear in her expression.

Catherine sighed and sank down in her chair. "Guests are fleeing the house as if their lives depend on it."

"They were trying to be considerate," Lady Ashton said unconvincingly. "It was kind of Ruth to try and make more room for other people."

"Aunt Ruth has never thought about another person in her life," Catherine retorted, drawing a warning snort from her father. She smiled apologetically. "I only mean that Aunt Ruth and her daughters expect luxury. Surely, they know Ridgewick Hall is nicer than the local Inn. What does it say about this house that they are willingly choosing to stay there instead?"

"It says nothing about this house," Lady Ashton said, standing up. She placed her hands on her hips, though her shoulders seemed more stooped than usual, as though standing up tall was too much work. "If people want to connect two unrelated events that have occurred here to try and say anything about the safety of our home, that is their own problem. We know the truth."

Referring to Edward's murder of Mr. Matcham as an "event" was the most I'd heard Lady Ashton speak of the crime. She kept glancing at her husband nervously, no doubt wondering how he was doing. Lord Ashton did not discuss the matter. Not even indirectly. And since we'd arrived at Ridgewick Hall for the first time since the crime, he had hardly discussed anything at all.

"What is the truth?" Alice asked, forehead wrinkled in confusion.

"That the house is safe!" Lady Ashton stamped her foot. "Ridgewick Hall is safe, and no one has any reason to worry at all."

Suddenly, there was another knock on the doors to the sitting room, and Lady Ashton spun on her heel. "Who is it now? Should we offer everyone on the estate access to our private family conversation?"

Alice giggled at her mother's outburst, and Catherine dropped her face in her hands in embarrassment. Then, the doors opened and a police sergeant stepped inside. Lady Ashton's face went pink at once. "I'm sorry, Sergeant."

"Quite alright," the man said, removing his hat and holding it against his stomach with folded hands.

"How can we help you?" Lord Ashton stood up and

moved to stand next to his wife, though he kept a safe distance between them so they did not touch.

The sergeant was a middle-aged man with a thick mustache and pale green eyes. He worked his lips together nervously, the mustache bobbing side to side like a boat in choppy waters. "Is it all right to talk here?"

"Yes," Lady Ashton said. "This is my family. There are no secrets between us."

I felt my cheeks redden slightly. I certainly had more than my fair share of secrets.

The sergeant pushed the door closed and stepped more fully into the room. "I will cut to the chase, then. No one will be allowed to leave this house or the village until Augusta Whitlock's cause of death has been determined."

There was a long stretch of silence where everyone stared at the sergeant, waiting for him to continue explaining the situation. He didn't, however. He just stared back at us.

"What do you mean?" Lady Ashton finally asked. "She was an old woman. She died."

"She did," the Sergeant said with a brisk nod. "And the circumstances of her death have yet to be determined."

Catherine sat forward and shook her head. "I don't understand. I am getting married in three days. I have to leave this house. We have a trip planned."

"We apologize for any inconvenience this may cause."

"Natural causes." Lady Ashton said the words as though trying to convince herself that she had actually heard them. "Her death was due to natural causes. That is what we were told. It is what Dr. Shaw determined."

"Further investigation has caused us to change the cause of death. It is now viewed as suspicious."

Lord Ashton's face was paler than I'd ever seen it, and he did not look at anyone as the news was delivered. Lady Ashton tried to catch his eye, but eventually turned to stare at her daughters. Alice was wide-eyed and quiet, for once. Catherine looked once again on the verge of tears. And no one was saying anything. I sat forward and raised my hand slightly, drawing the sergeant's attention.

"Excuse me, Sergeant, but why exactly is her death considered suspicious?"

He sighed, as though he had far too much going on to waste time explaining the details to me. "After her body was collected, a brief examination was carried out that revealed details consistent with a suspicious death. Then, interviews with several of the party guests revealed behavior that the coroner believes points to a possible homicide."

Lady Ashton gasped and clapped a hand over her mouth.

"Could you elaborate on those details?" I asked.

The sergeant shook his head, mustache twitching. "I'm sorry. I cannot say any more."

"When will we be able to leave?" Catherine asked, glancing back at Charles, who was rubbing his hand up and down her back reassuringly.

"I do not know. I'm sorry." The sergeant took a step back towards the door, clearly ready to leave. "The house will be monitored by officers to ensure no one leaves."

Just as he spoke, something caught my eye, and I turned to see Aunt Ruth and her daughters being escorted back up the main walkway to the house, an officer trailing behind them. Aunt Ruth's face was red and pursed, and her daughters looked noticeably less chipper than usual. The driver was pulling their luggage from the car and setting it in the grass. Clearly, they were not going to be allowed to leave as planned.

Lady Ashton followed the sergeant from the room, asking him more questions as he tried to leave. Alice jumped up to follow.

"I can't believe this," Catherine said to Charles, her eyes wide and glassy with tears. "This can't be happening."

"It will all work out," Charles whispered back, smoothing a hand across Catherine's hair tenderly.

I looked away, feeling strange about interrupting what appeared to be a private moment, but I also didn't want to go into the entryway where I could hear Lady Ashton talking with the Sergeant and Aunt Ruth arguing with the officers. The house was descending into chaos, and I needed a moment to process the information.

Augusta Whitlock had been murdered. Probably.

The fact that she had dropped dead in the middle of a party with no obvious injuries to her body suggested poison, but without more information from the Sergeant or the coroner, I couldn't be certain.

"It won't work out," Catherine said, folding her hands nervously in her lap. "Everything is ruined. We won't be able to go to the chapel to be married, and even if we do, we won't be able to leave on our honeymoon. The entire trip will be spoiled."

If the police were keeping all of the guests at the

house, it meant they suspected someone inside the house to be guilty, which made the most sense. And if that was true, the number of suspects was small. Plus, there were only a few people with any noteworthy connection to Augusta Whitlock, which narrowed the scope even more.

"The police will solve the case," Charles soothed.

"What if they don't?" Catherine asked.

I ran through the suspects in my mind, barely hearing their conversation. Nicholas Whitlock stood the most to gain from his grandmother's death, but he was also the most devastated by her loss. Based upon the little I'd known of Augusta, she likely had a great number of enemies, but over the course of the weekend, she had made two: Miss Brown and Lady Harwood.

Suddenly, Catherine was standing in front of me. I startled and looked up.

"I've been trying to capture your attention," Catherine said, kneeling in front of me. "Will you help?"

"Help with what?" I asked, still dazed and half in my own thoughts.

"The investigation," she said. "I trust you more than any detective, Rose, and I believe you can solve this case before the wedding."

"If there is a case to solve at all," Charles added. "It might be that the coroner's determination is wrong, and the woman really did die of old age."

"Either way, Rose can uncover the truth," Catherine said over her shoulder. She turned back to me and gripped my hands. "You have solved cases like this before, and you saved Charles' life in New York City. If anyone is capable of finding the murderer, you are."

"Thank you for your faith," I said. "But it seems the police are taking a strong lead on this. I'm not sure my skills will be required."

"Please, Rose." Catherine's blue eyes were cutting, pleading. The stress of the wedding and the past few weeks had worn on her. She was rawer than I'd ever seen her, and the idea of refusing her request and standing by while her wedding and plans were ruined seemed unconscionable.

I could hear Lady Ashton pleading with her husband in the entrance hall to speak with the Sergeant while also trying to calm Aunt Ruth, who could not understand why she was being held prisoner when she had done nothing wrong. I realized that Catherine wasn't the only person who needed this case solved. Everyone was overwhelmed, and everyone needed closure. And whether I would be successful or not, I didn't know, but it felt like my duty to try and do what I could.

I turned back to Catherine, squeezed her hands, and nodded. "I will do my best."

11

Nicholas was on the terrace when Lord and Lady Ashton informed him of the coroner's conclusion. He'd spent several hours after his grandmother's death shut away in his room, but as he calmed down and the day wore on, he'd moved out to the terrace. From his vantage point, it was possible to see the depression in the grass where Aunt Augusta had fallen and where the doctors and officers had knelt down around her. Servants were picking up what remained of the garden party after the police had combed the area for clues.

As soon as the news was delivered, the sound of his weeping once again filled the house.

Lord Ashton came back inside several minutes later, shaking his head.

"How is he taking the news?" Charles Barry asked, his hand perched on the back of the sofa. The rest of the wedding guests had been gathered in the sitting room to have the full situation explained to them. Aside from Aunt Ruth and her daughters, everyone was responding surprisingly well to the news of their temporary captivity within the estate. No one had begun to suspect one another of the crime yet, though I knew that moment would come sooner rather than later.

"How does it sound like he is taking it?" Lord Ashton asked, gesturing towards the terrace doors and then dropping down into a chair in the corner. He turned towards the window without saying anything else.

"I should have stayed with her," Nicholas cried, his voice muffled, presumably in Lady Ashton's shoulder. "I left her side and opened the door for someone to get close to her and harm her. This is all my fault."

Everyone remained quiet while Nicholas sobbed. Alice stood near the terrace door, her ear pressed towards the crack to better hear Nicholas. She had changed into a black, long-sleeved dress, and had done her best to stay close to Nicholas throughout the day. She was terribly concerned about him.

Catherine and Charles stayed close together in the corner, whispering back and forth. Catherine was clearly concerned about how the events would unfold and whether her wedding or honeymoon would happen at all, but I also couldn't help but notice how much more at ease she seemed. Now that there were no more events or parties to plan and execute, she smiled on rare occasion and didn't flit around the house like an agitated bird.

Once the crying from the terrace began to fade, Lady Ashton led Nicholas Whitlock into the sitting room, her arm around his shoulders. Alice extended a hand as if to comfort him or escort him in some way, but when Lady Ashton and Nicholas moved past her without a second glance, her arm fell to her side and she returned to her post next to the door. Vivian Barry stood and relinquished her seat to the mourning man, who dropped into it like a sack of bones, barely holding himself together at all. He sniffled and glanced up to take in everyone in the room.

"I'm sorry my grandmother's death has caused such an inconvenience for many of you," he started.

Vivian Barry waved away his concern and shook her head, but directly next to her, Aunt Ruth was nodding in agreement.

"But I'm sure the police will solve the case and have us all on our way soon," he finished, his voice growing thicker with every word. By the time he finished, his shoulders were shaking, and Lady Ashton was stooped over him, patting his back. He shook his head and lowered his face into his hands. "I cannot believe someone would want to hurt her. I can't understand it."

Everyone began to shift in their seats, uncomfortable, and within a few minutes, the room was cleared except for Nicholas and Lady Ashton, who had earned the unfortunate job of comforting the young man in his time of grief.

WHEN I RETURNED to my room, Alice was already sitting on the edge of the bed, her legs curled underneath her.

She looked up as I entered and then quickly back down at her hands.

I hesitated in the doorway. "I'm not sure Aunt Augusta's room has been cleared yet. The police may want to search it before her things are packed away."

Alice nodded, her lips twisted to the corner of her mouth while she bit the inside of her cheek.

I moved across the room and sat at the wooden chair in front of the desk. Alice had never been angry with me before. She'd been annoyed by me and Catherine, certainly, but in a loving way. This, however, was not loving. I'd genuinely hurt Alice's feelings, and now I had to try and rectify it.

"I was hoping I could ask for your help," I said. This was true. I had questions I needed answered about Nicholas and Augusta Whitlock, but I couldn't ask anyone else. I couldn't risk exposing my lack of knowledge on the family to anyone other than Alice. However, I also thought seeking Alice's assistance would flatter her into forgiving me.

Alice lifted her head as I spoke and quickly turned away, her chin jutted out. "I'm surprised you would need anything from me."

"Why is that?" I asked. "You've helped me a great deal over this last week."

"Have I?" she asked, mock surprise thick in her voice. "I thought all I'd done was relentlessly tease those around me. How wonderful to hear that was not the case and was, in fact, a severe exaggeration."

"Alice, I'm sorry I said that. It was hurtful and not at

all true." It was a little true, but that truth would make for a terrible apology.

"You called me spoiled," Alice said, turning to me, her brown curls tight around her face from the extra humidity in the air. "You made it seem as though I was incapable of being kind because of my wealth, when you yourself grew up wealthy. You are a hypocrite, Rose Beckingham."

Countless times since returning to London to be with the Beckinghams, I'd been faced with the reality of my situation. That I was not Rose Beckingham and knew almost nothing about their family or upbringing. Yet, I could not admit such a thing to Alice. I could not tell her that I had grown up poor and parentless. That I was still growing accustomed to the lavish lifestyle they led. So, I nodded.

"I was being a hypocrite, and I'm sorry. This wedding has everyone a little mad."

Alice groaned. "I will die of happiness when this wedding is finally over. I am so tired of discussing it."

Realizing what she had said, she smirked, holding in her laughter. "I suppose another death is the last thing this family needs."

"Especially Nicholas," I said, broaching the reason I'd come up to see her in the first place. "He is very upset about his grandmother."

Alice's face twisted into pity. "He is devastated. I feel so bad for him."

"How long had he been taking care of Aunt Augusta?"

"When we went on that walk the first day we arrived—"

She cut herself off and widened her eyes, grinning from ear to ear. "I was far too nervous to talk, so he carried the conversation, but he was so friendly, Rose. And sweet. But anyway, he told me he had been living with his grandmother exclusively for the last year. Her health has been declining steadily since then. He knew she didn't have much time left, but I'm sure he didn't foresee her passing away this weekend."

"Did he say what he was doing before he moved in with her?" I asked.

Alice shook her head. "He didn't say. Though, he did say that living with her was a large change from his usual lifestyle. Aunt Augusta didn't like to leave the house. It took him weeks to convince her to come to Catherine's wedding, which is, I'm sure, why he is feeling so guilty about everything. He is the reason she came here in the first place."

It seemed strange that Nicholas would care so much about a distant cousin's wedding. From the way it seemed, he had never been particularly close with the Beckinghams, so I had to wonder why he would spend weeks persuading his grandmother to come. Perhaps, after months of being alone with the old woman, he was desperate for any kind of human interaction.

"I can't imagine what it must have been like for him to be trapped inside with her for so long," Alice said, speaking my thoughts. "But according to him, she was very grateful for his assistance. She made him the sole heir to her fortune."

Alice turned to me, brow quizzical. "Didn't you need my help with something?"

"Oh, yes. This was it," I said. "I just had a few questions about Nicholas and Aunt Augusta."

She narrowed her eyes. "Why do you want to know so much about him?"

"His grandmother just died," I said with an innocent shrug. "If the police are saying she was murdered, I thought it would be good to know as much about him as I can. I couldn't ask your mother, so you were the next best option."

"Why couldn't you ask my mother?" Suddenly, I felt like I was the one being interrogated. Alice leaned forward on the bed, all of her focus on me.

Because I did not want her to realize how little I knew about the family. "She was busy."

I could tell Alice was still suspicious. Mostly because I knew she would never want to believe Nicholas could be capable of any crime, let alone murder. Her shoulders relaxed, and she waved a hand towards the door. "She is probably free now. She will have more answers for you than I do, I'm sure."

Deciding I'd pushed Alice far enough for one day, I thanked her and left to find Lady Ashton.

NICHOLAS HAD RETIRED to his room for the evening, too exhausted from crying to eat or attempt to talk to any of the other guests, so Lady Ashton was finally free of him and alone in the kitchen when I found her. She was picking at a tray of leftover desserts from the garden party.

"It seems impossible that the party could have been

only this afternoon," I said, knocking on the door to announce myself.

She looked up, her eyes wrinkled at the corners and weary. Still, she managed a small smile. "Doesn't it? It seems several days have been fit into this one. I am very ready for it to end."

I walked into the kitchen and leaned back against the countertop. The usual kitchen staff were not around, and I wondered whether everyone wasn't experiencing fatigue after the long day.

"Are you here for an evening snack like me?" Lady Ashton asked, gesturing to a plate of biscuits.

"Not exactly, though I am not one to turn down dessert," I said, grabbing a shortbread biscuit.

"A trait that runs in the family, I think." She took the last bite of a small cake and then wiped her hands together to get rid of the crumbs. "So, what can I do for you?"

"You have done enough this week that I hate to ask for anything else from you, but I wondered whether I couldn't ask you a few questions. About Nicholas."

"We are family," Lady Ashton emphasized, driving home the stake of guilt that was already burrowing into my stomach. "I am always here to help. You have done so much for our family, Rose."

I shook my head, but Lady Ashton crossed the small space between us, laying her hand on top of mine.

"Truly, Rose, you have taken care of my girls while their father and I dealt with the loss of Edward. You have been a bright spot in all of our lives, and I am so grateful that we've had this time together. I see you as one of my own children, rather than a niece."

My throat felt thick with unshed tears, and I swallowed back the emotion. "Thank you. I see all of you as family, as well. Dear, dear family."

Lady Ashton smiled and winked at me. Then, she leaned back against the counter and gestured for me to carry on.

"I only wonder how Nicholas Whitlock spent his time while I was away in India?" I asked. "Alice said Nicholas told her he'd been taking care of his grandmother for the last year, but what was he doing before that?"

Lady Ashton's eyes widened, and she shook her head. "I'm afraid it isn't a very nice story. Not one Aunt Augusta would want to hear me repeating."

Intrigue caused me to lean forward and lower my voice. "Does he have a criminal past?"

"Oh, no," Lady Ashton corrected quickly. "Not unless you count breaking hearts as a crime. The only thing our Nicholas Whitlock was guilty of was being a hopeless philanderer."

"Oh." It felt strange to be disappointed that the man wasn't a criminal. It would have made it much easier to solve the case if he had been.

"His mother, my cousin, died when he was barely eighteen. He inherited a deal of money from her, but not enough to sustain his lifestyle."

"And what lifestyle was that?" I asked.

"Drinking and women," she whispered. "He has also never minded a little luxury. He sold his mother's house for the money and spent it on fine hotel rooms and restaurants. When that ran out, he borrowed money. He even contacted me once about a small loan."

"Did he really?" I tried to imagine the Nicholas Whitlock I'd seen over the last few days—confident, charming, and, more recently, sobbing—begging anyone for money. I couldn't quite picture it.

"He did, though we do not hold it against him. He was young, and, as you know, every family has their own shameful past."

Lady Ashton truly had no idea exactly how well I knew that truth. I was now privy to the shames of several families—my own and Rose's. High or low born, everyone had a secret.

"So, once the money ran out and he'd cashed in on what little good will he had with his remaining family, it ended up that only Aunt Augusta was willing to take him in."

"I never viewed her as a particularly generous woman," I admitted.

Lady Ashton laughed. "And you'd be right not to. I tend to believe she found a kindred spirit in Nicholas. Not in the sense that she, too, owed many people money, but in that neither of them had anywhere to turn. Aunt Augusta had a bad habit of making enemies. She was estranged from her own daughter."

"Nicholas' mother?"

She nodded. "When his mother died, Aunt Augusta had not seen her in years. To my understanding, Nicholas barely knew his grandmother. It was desperation that brought him to her doorstep."

"And he left behind his old lifestyle in favor of caring

for an elderly woman? Forgive me, but I can't believe that was an easy transition for him to make. Not if he was truly as wild as you have made him seem."

"I may have even downplayed his lifestyle," Lady Ashton admitting with a scandalous smile. Then, she sobered. "His temperament did change drastically, though. In my opinion, Nicholas was searching for a purpose in life, and Aunt Augusta gave him that."

I grabbed another shortbread biscuit from the tray and took a small bite. They were stale, but still delicious.

"Who was caring for her before he came along?" I asked.

Lady Ashton frowned. "I'm not sure. I don't recall there being anyone. As Nicholas said the other day, Aunt Augusta kept very few servants. She did not trust anyone to be in her home or know too much about her life. Once Nicholas began caring for her, she became even more secretive and reclusive. We rarely saw her over this last year. It is why it was so alarming to see her in such a state of decline when they arrived."

"She was not always so ill?"

"No. In fact, she was remarkably hardy. Of course, when I remember her clearest was many years ago. A lot can change in that time. She was an old woman."

"True, but if the police are correct, her age had little to do with her death. Perhaps, her suspicions were not so misplaced. She had a very large fortune with no immediate heirs. Do you think it possible Nicholas could have seen an opportunity?"

Lady Ashton shook her head. "It is those very suspicions that I believe would have saved her from such a fate. She had a will, but I am certain that, as with every will she had written before, she kept it hidden away from everyone."

"She had multiple wills?"

"As I said, she had a bad habit of making enemies. She wrote her own daughter out of her will once they no longer had a relationship, and I'm sure she added Nicholas when he reentered her life," she said. "Aunt Augusta was a nervous, angry woman, and she did not trust anyone. She kept her will hidden so that if her worst nightmare came true and she was killed for her money, no one would inherit. Including Nicholas."

From the little I knew of Aunt Augusta, this way of handling her will seemed likely. Though, if that was the case, Nicholas would be foolish to kill her. Unless, of course, he knew where the will was.

"But Aunt Augusta had worried about people being after her for years. Just as Lady Harwood is afraid of illness, Aunt Augusta was afraid of greedy relatives, and I believe both of them wasted a lot of energy with useless worry."

"So, you do not believe the conclusion reached by the police?" I asked. "That she was murdered?"

Lady Ashton's mouth twisted in thought, and she looked so much like Alice it was uncanny. Then, she shook her head. "I can't say one way or the other for certain, but my instincts lead me to believe there has been some sort of misunderstanding. Simply put, the chances of more than one murder occurring in our house seem very low."

I could see the memory of Edward's crime on Lady

Ashton's face, and I reached out and laid my hand on hers, offering what little comfort I could.

"Stranger things have happened."

"Yes," she said, bobbing her head back and forth. "Though, if she truly was murdered, I will believe us to be the unluckiest family in the world."

12

Lady Ashton left shortly after our conversation to find her husband, making a subtle comment about him hiding away to avoid the drama. She said it with a smile, but I'd noticed her attempts to engage Lord Ashton over the few days we'd been at Ridgewick Hall, and I knew there was a hint of truth to her words. After she left, I ate yet another stale biscuit and then mounted the stairs to the second floor.

It was not late by any means, but everyone had retired to their own rooms earlier than normal. Partially to escape Nicholas' crying, but also because the day had been exhausting. The officers assigned to watch the house and keep the occupants on the property were visible from almost every window, and it was difficult to find anything suitable to talk about that didn't involve the death, possible murder, or the fact that everyone was trapped on the property until the case was solved. So, sleeping seemed easier.

The hallway was dim, only a few lamps along the

length of the corridor turned on. I could hear soft chatter behind some of the doors I passed. Alice seemed to have forgiven me for my outburst at the garden party, but I knew she would still push hard for her own room. As I told Alice, Aunt Augusta's room should remain undisturbed until the police had a chance to search it, but I decided to look in on the room quickly just to be sure. If her things had already been removed, then there was no reason for me not to sleep there for the night. Aside from the obvious discomfort associated with sleeping in the bed of a recently deceased woman.

Aunt Augusta's room had been at the far end of a narrow corridor. Aside from the guest room, the hallway housed a bathroom, library, and private office where Lord Ashton spent many of his daytime hours. At night, Aunt Augusta was alone in the hallway due to Lady Ashton strategically placing her as far away from the other guests as possible.

Since no one else was staying down that way, it was dark when I turned the corner. A little light filtered in from the main hallway, but it dissipated quickly, and by the time I reached the midway point, I had to stop and blink to let my eyes adjust to the darkness.

I found the door and had to run my hand across the wood to locate the handle. When I did, the door pushed inward without resistance. It had already been opened. This didn't alarm me at all, as no one was staying in the room any longer, so I pushed it open the rest of the way and stepped inside.

The room had a similar layout to my own, though slightly smaller. The bed was pushed against the wall to the left with a dresser and armoire on the opposite wall. A small writing desk was stationed in front of the windows. I saw all of this clearly because the curtains had been pulled back to let in the light of the full moon. Compared to the dark hallway, the room was almost bright, making it easy to see the dark figure silhouetted against the windows, head lowered to read something in their hands.

"Nicholas?" I recognized the build of Augusta's grandson immediately, and my heart lurched in my chest.

He spun around, startled by my presence, but rather than looking guilty or suspicious as I expected, he chuckled to himself, a hand placed on his chest. "You scared me, Rose. I didn't hear you approaching. I suppose my attention was consumed by this letter."

"I'm sorry," I said, wondering if I wasn't apologizing to a murderer. "What are you doing in here?"

He sighed and dropped the paper on top of a stack of papers. Then, he turned and rested on the edge of the desk, arms folded across his chest. He was already in his pajamas, though he didn't seem to mind me seeing him in them. "I couldn't sleep, and I thought I should start the process of clearing out her things. For a week in the country, my grandmother travelled with a great deal of personal belongings. I'm already dreading the process of clearing out her house."

"I'm sorry," I apologized again, unsure what to say.

"It will be difficult," he said, his voice breaking slightly around the words. "I count myself lucky to be one of the few people in this world she was close to, but it does mean I will carry most of the burden to sort through her things on my own."

"I'm not sure how much longer I will be in London, but should you need anything, I would be more than willing to help in any way I can." This was close to the last thing I wanted to do for many reasons. Not least of which was that I suspected Nicholas could be guilty of the crime of killing the woman whose belongings he now needed to sort through. Still, it seemed the right thing to do was to offer my assistance.

"Thank you," he said genuinely, taking a step closer to me. I wanted to back away, but it seemed rude. "I know we are not actually family, Rose. Not in the blood sense, anyway. But I think of you as family now. The offer of help goes both ways. Should you ever need anything, feel free to reach out to me."

I smiled up at him, hoping it looked more natural than it felt. "Thank you, Nicholas. That means a great deal."

He nodded and then seemed to be waiting for me to leave, so he could return to what he was doing, however, I stayed put. We stared at one another for another couple of seconds before Nicholas tilted his head to the side and narrowed his eyes. "Is there anything you are looking for exactly?"

"Oh, no," I said quickly. "I actually came down to check whether the police had inspected this room yet. Alice is anxious to have her own space again, and I offered to sleep here now that Aunt Augusta...no longer needs the room."

"The police?" Nicholas asked, eyebrows drawn together.

My eyes were adjusting to the light in the room, but with him standing where he was a dark shadow was cast across his face, making his expression look more ominous than confused.

"Well, since the police believe the death may not have been natural," I said as gently as I could to avoid another break down, "I assumed they would search through her things for any possible clues."

His mouth parted in surprise, and he pushed away from the desk as though just leaning on it was polluting the scene. "I hadn't even considered that."

"It may be wise to talk to the police before you begin going through her things," I said. "Just as a precaution."

"Of course. I can't believe I didn't think of that." He turned back to the desk, shuffled the papers into a neat stack, and then rushed from the room and into the hallway. I followed after him, closing the door behind me. "Hopefully I have not ruined any evidence. I would hate to think I kept the person involved from being captured."

"I'm sure everything will be fine," I said.

Nicholas expressed several more times that he had not even considered that his grandmother's room could have been part of the investigation before he finally said goodnight and walked down the hallway in the direction of his own room.

I walked slowly towards the room I was sharing with Alice, waiting for the definitive click of Nicholas' door closing before I began walking at a normal pace. Just as I passed Lady Harwood's door, however, it opened and Dr.

Shaw stepped out, black medical bag in hand. He startled at the sight of me.

"Apologies," I said. "That is the second time I've done that to someone tonight. Apparently, I should walk with a heavier footfall."

"Quite alright," Dr. Shaw said, barely managing a grimace at my attempt at humor. He tipped his head to me. "Goodnight, Miss Beckingham."

He moved to walk past me, but I followed after him. "Actually, Dr. Shaw, do you have a moment?"

He looked regretfully towards his door just next door, and I knew he was probably as tired as everyone else— perhaps even more so since he had the task of caring for Lady Harwood, who had been anxious all day about the possibility that she could contract whatever mysterious illness had killed Augusta Whitlock. Finally, he turned back to me and folded his hands in front of him, the bag banging against his thighs. "Of course, Miss Beckingham. How can I help?"

"You examined Augusta Whitlock, correct?"

His shoulders lifted slightly as though he was shielding himself. "I did."

"And you believed her death to be from natural causes?"

"I did. I was honest in my assessment and had no reason to believe she was suffering from anything other than ill health," he said. "It was obvious to everyone that her health was failing from the moment she arrived at the estate, so I counted her pale complexion, dizzy spells, and chills and fevers as normal for her. I never suspected for a moment it could have been from poison."

"Poison?" I asked, taking a step closer to the doctor and lowering my voice. "Do the police believe she was poisoned?"

Dr. Shaw looked around nervously, clearly trying to decide whether he had said too much or whether he should be alone with me in the hallway. I was far too concerned about his answer to my question to be concerned with decency or something as trivial as personal space. "That is my understanding. I am not being consulted on the case, so I cannot say for certain either way. I only know that the evidence they have and my description of her symptoms led them to the conclusion of homicide."

Questions swirled around my mind. If Augusta Whitlock arrived at the estate suffering the symptoms of a possible poisoning then she would have had to have been poisoned prior to her arrival. Though, thinking back to the first day I met her in the back garden, I couldn't remember her stumbling or seeming especially ill. She had on a thick velvet dress, which I found odd given the heat, but I didn't really begin to notice her symptoms worsening until the morning of her argument with Miss Brown.

"Do they know when she could have been poisoned?" I asked. "Or how? Was it a slow-acting poison or one that would take effect immediately?"

Dr. Shaw took another step away from me, his long, gaunt face growing paler with each word I spoke. He shook his head. "I really do not know, Miss Beckingham. You will need to speak to the police, though it is my understanding that they are not sharing many details since the killer has not yet been captured."

I nodded and tried to ease back. Dr. Shaw looked moments away from running down the hallway, and I didn't want to scare him away. Not when he could be a useful source of information later. Still, I had to wonder what he thought about his employer. Lady Harwood had been in an argument with the deceased moments before her death. I didn't pretend to assume Lady Harwood travelled with poison hidden in her pocket, but Dr. Shaw's medical bag had not been too far away. Perhaps, she had snuck something out of it.

Just as I was about to casually bring up the matter, Lady Harwood herself called to Dr. Shaw from her room. "Dr. Shaw? Is that you in the hallway?"

Dr. Shaw looked at me as though he blamed me for him having to go back into the lady's room. He quietly excused himself and stepped inside.

"Oh, good," Lady Harwood said, her voice muffled through the door. "Could you take my temperature one more time? I'm feeling feverish."

CATHERINE'S WEDDING was in two more days. I had two days to solve this murder before it effectively ruined her big day and her honeymoon. Two days to sort through a lifetime of family history and an entire household's worth of motive. The truth was, no matter who was my main suspect, anyone could have done it. Sane people liked to look for reason and logic in murder, but murderers were rarely concerned with being rational. The act of murder itself proved that the person who committed it was acting beyond the bounds of normal human behavior. So, how then, were normal humans meant to solve the crimes?

Miss Brown was a possibility. She had been fired the day before the old woman's death, and in the days preceding, Aunt Augusta had worked Miss Brown to the bone. Was it possible she had grown tired of the old woman's demands and set out to kill her? It could have been out of frustration or, based on her lingering stares at the old woman's grandson, it could have been out of love. Perhaps, Miss Brown wanted to free Nicholas Whitlock from the hold of his grandmother's illness? It was possible, but the poison she administered would have had to be slow-acting since she was not present at the time of the death.

Lady Harwood was another possibility, as she too had argued with the deceased, but her motive would have been born from the heat of the moment. She would have needed to have poison on hand that she could administer quickly without anyone noticing. It seemed far-fetched, though, as I'd told Lady Ashton, stranger things had happened.

Nicholas Whitlock seemed the most likely suspect, though if Lady Ashton was correct, he would not inherit anything since Augusta Whitlock kept her will in a secret location. So, the murder would have been committed out of sheer hatred rather than any hope of gain. Unless, of course, he had the will, which was something I desperately needed to know.

Possibilities swirled around my head as I walked back

to the room Alice and I shared. Perhaps, Charles Barry was so determined to stop Catherine's wedding to another Charles that he killed one of the guests to halt the proceedings. If so, he chose the incorrect guest. No one would particularly miss the old woman's meanness. Except for Nicholas, apparently.

I pushed open the door to our room slowly, not wanting to wake Alice if she was already asleep, but as soon as the door opened, I noticed the lamp over the desk was on. Alice was sitting at the wooden chair in front of the desk, one leg crossed over the other, her hands perched on her knees. She was staring at the door, her expression blank.

I smiled nervously and closed the door behind me. "What is it, Alice? Why aren't you in bed?"

"I am not a child," she snapped, making me wonder whether our argument from earlier in the day wasn't behind us, after all. "I can choose to go to bed when I'd like."

"All right." I moved to the dresser and pulled out my dressing gown. "You do what you'd like, but I am going to go to sleep. Today has been a very long, stressful day. I think we could all use the rest."

"I know." The two words were sharp and clear, and I stood tall and turned around to look at my youngest cousin. I narrowed my eyes, trying to decide if she was responding to my statement or making one of her own.

"What?" I asked.

Alice stood up and crossed the room slowly, her brown eyes never leaving mine. It was unsettling, the way she was staring at me. I couldn't move or speak. It felt as though I was being hypnotized. Alice stopped just in front of me, and I realized for the first time that she was the same height as me. When I'd arrived almost a year before, she'd barely reached my nose, and now we stood nose to nose.

"I know," she repeated.

I shook my head, still confused.

"I know," she said for the third time. "That you are not really Rose Beckingham."

The room seemed to spin around me, and I reached out for something to hold me steady. Alice grabbed my arm, holding me upright, her brown eyes still locking me into place.

13

I released my hold on her forearm and took a step back, trying my best to smile. To pretend like this was some kind of funny joke.

"What are you talking about, Alice?" I asked, turning to grab my nightgown from the dresser and walking over to the bed. My legs were trembling, and I hoped my dress was hiding it well enough that she wouldn't notice.

"I remember when you first arrived in London," Alice said evenly. "Edward had suspicions from the moment you arrived. I overheard him talking to Catherine shortly after you came to stay with us about how different you seemed. You had a scar, of course, so you looked different, but he said there was something off about your manner, too. Catherine reminded him you'd just been through a tragedy, so your personality would likely be changed forever, but Edward thought there was something more. He suspected you were an imposter only here to collect on Rose's inheritance."

I laid the nightgown out on the bed and made like I

was going to change into my bed clothes, but I couldn't control my hands anymore. I had no choice but to sit on the edge of the bed to keep from falling over. What was happening? How did Alice know? And how could I convince her she was wrong?

Alice walked across the room and sat on the edge of the bed, looking at me even though I refused to meet her eyes. I kept my gaze on the striped-pattern of the bedspread.

"I thought Edward was only upset because he would no longer inherit your family's fortune. The rest of us, myself included, were just happy to hear you were alive. That someone had survived. So, I didn't put much stock in his theory. Neither, it seems, did Catherine."

"Good," I said, finally finding my voice. "Because it is madness. I know things with Edward were complex, and I do not wish to speak ill of the dead, but he was not a man of sound mind, Alice. Not at the end, at least. I do not think he should be trusted."

"What of me, Rose?" Alice asked. "Am I of sound mind?"

She sounded so grown up compared to the young girl I had first met. In that moment, she did not seem silly or naïve or immature. She sounded like an adult, and when I finally met her eyes, I could not bring myself to lie to her. So, I said nothing.

"Because I am beginning to have my doubts," she admitted. "You were in India for many years, that is true, but you lived in London for ten years before that. There are people you grew up with who you have no recollection of. You don't recognize members of your own family or know anything about our family history. It is as if your time in India washed away everything before it."

I could not breathe or move or speak. I had no defense. No way to justify the gaps in my knowledge. I'd used Alice as a reference book for the Beckingham family, and it had cost me dearly. She was not the unobservant, self-absorbed girl I'd thought. Alice Beckingham, for all her love of gossip, paid attention. I only wished I'd paid better attention myself.

"All of those things alone do not necessarily mean anything," Alice said. "But together? They paint a distressing picture. Rose, or...whoever you may be. I just want to know the truth."

The truth. I wasn't certain I knew the truth anymore. One thing I did know, however, was that guilt had been wrenching my insides for weeks. Ever since I returned to New York City to be with Alice and Catherine, I'd felt the urge to tell them all the truth. To reveal my deception and come clean. And since arriving in London, seeing Lord and Lady Ashton together, seeing them so excited to see me again—it made me miserable to think that I had fooled them. To think there was a possibility that their love for me was nothing more than obligation. That the family I'd come to view as my own might not feel the same way if they knew everything.

The only truth I knew was that I could no longer live in the lie. One way or another, it all would have come out eventually, and Alice was simply shortening my timeline. So, I looked up at her, tears brimming at the edges of my eyes, and told her what she wanted to know.

"I'm Nellie Dennet."

Alice seemed to sag under my admission, as though she hadn't actually believed her theory was true until that moment. Her eyes went wide, and she stared at me as I began to confess my real identity and my deeds. Everything I'd done and why.

"My intentions were not malicious," I said. "I did not and do not have any desire to harm anyone. I worked as Rose's companion in India. I took care of her needs and kept her company. I was in the car the day it exploded, and I was the only one to survive. In the hospital, someone misidentified me as Rose, and I did not correct them. I realized quickly that I had no one in the world to depend on. Without the Beckinghams, I would have been alone in the world, homeless and destitute, so I did what I needed to do to survive. Then, I realized that I could use Rose's inheritance to search for a missing relative. Living with you all was supposed to be temporary. I never intended to stay forever."

"You were going to use us?" Alice asked. There was a hint of betrayal in her voice, but mostly curiosity. Alice loved a good story, and who had a better one than I did?

I nodded. "I'm sorry, but that was before I knew you. Once I met you all, I loved you at once. I did eventually find my missing relative, but he was nothing like what I remembered, and I couldn't bear the thought of never seeing you and your family again, so I kept my secret."

"Is that why you left with Achilles?" she asked. "You went travelling with him to get away from us?"

"I needed time and space to think. To formulate a plan," I said. "But then Catherine messaged me to ask for help, and I couldn't refuse. I had to come back."

Alice listened and asked questions, probing deeper into my past. She did not display a great amount of emotion, but instead treated the conversation as an interrogation. I did my best to answer everything in full, explaining my thinking as best I could, having no idea how it would all end. I did, however, hold back from sharing the full details surrounding my unhappy reunion with my criminal brother, something that might be an insensitive topic, given the way it related to the loss of Alice's own brother Edward.

Would Alice run from the room and tell her family about my lies at once? Would she hate me? Or be afraid of me? I had no way to know or control how everything would turn out, so I simply did my best to be honest for what felt like the first time in a very long time.

"What is your plan now?" Alice asked. "You tried to travel and run away, but now you've come back. What is next?"

I nervously played with the hem of my dress and shook my head. "I'm not sure, Alice. The only thing I know is that I love you and your family. I don't have anyone else in the world. I don't have anywhere to go. But I will not stay here if I'm not wanted. If you want me to tell everyone at once and leave, I will."

Alice pinched her lips together in thought and then shook her head. "That isn't what I want."

We sat in silence for several seconds, neither of us sure what to say when, finally, Alice laughed.

I looked up, surprised by the outburst, and Alice just smiled and shook her head. "I'm not sure why I feel uncomfortable. You are still the same person I've known for the last year. Rose Beckingham or not, you are still *Rose*. You are still the cousin I know and have come to love."

The emotion I'd been holding back threatened to spill over. I blinked away tears and swallowed back a lump in my throat.

"I love you like a sister, Rose. And I will keep your secret as long as you need me to. Though," she said, tilting her head to the side, eyebrows raised. "I think everyone else deserves to know eventually. They may even surprise you and not be too upset."

I wanted to believe Alice was right, but it was difficult to imagine they would respond as well as she had. Still, I smiled. "I will tell everyone eventually, but I don't want to ruin Catherine's wedding."

"Any more than it has already been ruined, you mean?" Alice asked, almost laughing.

"Exactly," I said. "I just need a bit more time."

Alice leaned across the bed and pulled me into a hug, her thin arms wrapped around my shoulders. "Take all the time you need. I'll be here."

14

Alice and I stayed up far too late chatting to be prepared when Catherine barged into our room just after dawn. She threw the door open and flung herself at my side of the bed, her palms pressing into the mattress so I almost rolled onto the floor. I yelped and scrambled into a sitting position as Alice groaned.

"What is going on?" she asked, squinting with one eye, the covers still pulled up to her shoulders.

"You have to get downstairs," Catherine said. She still had her nightgown on, and her blonde hair was pinned down into finger curls against her scalp.

"I'm in my nightgown," I said. "And so are you. You shouldn't be wandering around the house."

"Yes, what if Charles sees you?" Alice asked sleepily. I smiled at the fact that she could still manage to tease her sister while she was half-asleep.

Catherine leaned forward, putting even more weight on the bed and forcing me to scoot closer to Alice who nudged me with her elbow back onto my side of the bed. "The police sergeant is here."

"This early?" I asked. That seemed odd, though not a reason for panic.

"He is interviewing the servants," she said. "You should be down there to hear what they say. It could help your investigation."

"I'm sure the police won't allow me to sit in on their interview," I said. "I can interview the staff separately later."

Catherine shook her head. "There is no time. My wedding is in two days, Rose. Besides, the staff will be more forthcoming with the police than with you. For all they know, you could be the murderer."

"They do not suspect me."

Catherine raised her eyebrows. "Why wouldn't they? No one knows who did it. It could be anyone. Unless, of course, you've found an important clue that points to someone in particular?"

I bit the corner of my mouth and looked away from her. "I don't have much to go off of yet."

"Then you have to go downstairs," Catherine said, almost begging now.

I didn't want to go downstairs and insert myself into the interviews, but I also didn't want to let Catherine down. She was distressed, and her plan wasn't entirely without merit. I could learn some valuable information that might help point me in the right direction.

So, despite the exhaustion that kept my eyes half-closed, I put on a wool skirt with a white blouse and sweater, powdered my face, and adjusted my curls.

Catherine stood in the doorway the entire time, as though she didn't trust I would go downstairs if she left.

"This wedding has gone to your head, Catherine," Alice said from beneath the covers. "You have become far too bossy."

Catherine ignored her sister and saw me to the top of the stairs before she darted back into her own room.

I didn't hear the sergeant's voice until I reached the entrance hall. The staff was being interviewed in the formal sitting room at the front of the house. The doors were half-closed, allowing me only a sliver of a view into the room, but their voices drifted out clearly. He was speaking with George, Lord and Lady Ashton's driver.

"And you have worked for Lord and Lady Ashton for awhile now?" the sergeant asked.

"Yes, sir," George said. "I worked for them for many years, and then briefly worked for their niece, Miss Rose Beckingham, before returning to work for the Beckinghams."

George made no mention of the fact that he was fired from his position as the Beckingham's driver due to their suspicion that he was a criminal. I could not blame him for omitting that detail. He was innocent, as it turned out, so it seemed self-sabotaging to mention it.

"For James and Eleanor Beckingham?" the Sergeant clarified.

"Yes, Lord and Lady Ashton," George said.

"Would it be safe to assume you've met a great deal of their family members over the years?" he asked.

George hummed in the affirmative. "I've driven many of their family around London or delivered Lord and

Lady Ashton to their homes for a visit. I don't often speak with them on a personal basis, but I recognize many of them."

"And did you recognize Augusta Whitlock when she arrived?"

"I had never seen her before the day she arrived here at Ridgewick," George said. "I'd heard her name plenty, but she was not a regular visitor to the Beckingham home."

"When you heard her name, what was the context?" the Sergeant asked. "Were Lord and Lady Ashton fond of Augusta Whitlock?"

There was a long pause, and I pressed myself closer to the wall next to the door, aching to hear his answer. Finally, George sighed. "Truly, not many people spoke favorably of Augusta Whitlock. I do not wish to speak ill of the dead, but from the little I knew her these last few days, she was confrontational."

"She fought with the other guests?"

"Yes," George said.

"Did any of these fights stand out as particularly noteworthy?"

"As a matter of fact," George said. I heard his chair squeak as he leaned forward. "Lady Ashton assigned her servant to watch after Augusta Whitlock, and it did not end well. Mrs. Whitlock accused the servant of stealing from her."

"Did she steal from her?" the sergeant asked.

"A necklace was found in her room," George said, his voice sounding unconvinced. "I've known Miss Brown for a year, and she was always a sweet, quiet woman. Nothing had ever gone missing before this weekend, so it seemed surprising to me. Though, I was also surprised when Miss Brown was dismissed by Lady Ashton for the theft. She raised her voice to Lady Ashton and threatened Augusta Whitlock."

I had to cover my mouth to conceal a gasp. How had I forgotten that detail? Miss Brown's parting words before leaving the property had been a threat. *If I have anything to say about it, this will be the last time you treat anyone this way.*

"She threatened her? How?"

George spoke in a higher pitch than normal to mimic Miss Brown's voice. "If I have anything to say about it, this will be the last time you treat anyone this way."

"Did she say anything else?"

"I believe she also called the woman 'horrid,'" he said.

The Sergeant hummed, and I could hear the scratch of his pen across paper, taking notes. "But Miss Brown was dismissed from her duties, yes?"

"Yes," George said. "But I did see her on the property the day of Augusta Whitlock's death."

I froze to the spot, my heart practically leaping from my chest. How was I just now hearing about this?

"What was she doing here?" the Sergeant asked.

"I'm not sure," George admitted. "I didn't speak to her. I saw her from afar. Everyone was on the lawn for the party, and I saw her walk in a side door into the kitchen. I made to follow her and see why she'd returned, but then Augusta Whitlock fell and the screams from the lawn distracted me. I didn't see her again."

"You haven't seen her since that day?"

George made a noise in the back of his throat that sounded like a denial. "No, I haven't."

The interview began wrapping up, and I knew I could not be found standing outside the door. Besides, the information George had shared was enough that I didn't need to listen to any more interviews. Miss Brown threatening the deceased the day before her death was troubling, but did not necessarily connect her to the murder. However, now that she was also placed at the scene of the crime the day it occurred, there was no denying that she had moved up on the suspect list.

I crept out of the entrance hall and down the narrow hallway where the staff quarters were located.

Miss Brown's door was closed and there was no light coming from underneath the door, so I quietly turned the handle and stepped inside. One panel of the curtain was pulled back, allowing muted light from the sunrise to filter into the room, and enough light to see by.

I'd thoroughly searched Miss Brown's room a few days earlier, so I noticed, at once, that there were things missing that had been there when she'd stormed out. The Bible next to her bed, for one, was no longer there. Gone, too, were the few plain dresses she'd had hanging in her closet and the shoes beneath them. I didn't know whether Lady Ashton had ordered her things to be packed away or whether Miss Brown had come back to the house to collect them herself. Perhaps, that was why she'd returned to the house the day of the garden party.

Just as I had during the first search of her room, I looked under the bed and under the neatly tucked covers of her bed. I ran my hand along the baseboard and the cracks of the wooden floor, searching for any floorboards that would lift or hiding places we had missed on the initial search. I found nothing. There was a hairbrush that looked like it had fallen to the floor from the top of the dresser and slid beneath the night stand, but beyond that, the room was clean. Desperate for any kind of clue that could connect Miss Brown to Aunt Augusta's death, I crawled into the closet.

There were a few crates stacked in the corner that looked like they had been there for years and were labeled as seasonal decorations, but before I could open them, I noticed a thin layer of dust on the left side of the closet. The rest of the closet was slightly dusty, but this powder had a different appearance. It was white with a slight shimmer to it.

I did not recall noticing it the first time we were in the room, though I was not the one who searched the closet. Lady Ashton had taken on that task, and the shoe prints appeared to match the high-heels Lady Ashton most often wore—Miss Brown was usually seen in flats. If the footprints were truly Lady Ashton's, then it meant the dust was present before Miss Brown was dismissed from her duties.

I leaned forward, my nose almost touching the floor, and smelled the powder. There was no noticeable odor. Then, I ran my fingertips through it. The powder clung to my skin easily. The particles were incredibly fine and even the slightest exhale sent them wafting in the air like a puff of smoke. Perhaps it was makeup? A pressing powder of some kind? Even so, I couldn't imagine why it would be in the closet.

I was still kneeling in the closet when I heard the hinge of the bedroom door squeak open. I jumped to my feet immediately and spun around to find Nicholas Whitlock slowly closing the door to Miss Brown's room.

He was dressed and ready for the day in brown wool pants, a tan jacket, and a striped collared shirt beneath. His hair was dark and slicked to the side. Still, his shoulders were hunched as he moved, as though he was trying to make himself smaller than he really was, and his shoes stepped lightly. I knew at once he did not know I was in the room with him.

"Nicholas?"

His spine lengthened in an instant, and he jumped backwards in surprise, his legs hitting the edge of Miss Brown's bedside table. The lamp teetered dangerously but did not fall.

"Miss Beckingham," he said, hand to his chest, his breathing coming in fits and starts. "What are you doing in here, Rose?"

I brushed my hands on the fabric of my skirt, cleaning my fingers of the powder. "I believe I could ask you the same question."

Nicholas stared at me for a moment before he smiled. "I suppose you are right. Though, truthfully, I believe I know why you are here."

I narrowed my eyes. "You do?"

He nodded and took a step towards me. The room was already small, but with his broad shoulders filling the space, I felt even more crowded. Trapped.

"I've heard from a few of the other guests that you solved the last murder that occurred in this house," he said softly, taking another silent step towards me. "I suspect you are attempting to do the same thing again."

I was in Miss Brown's room pursuing her as a suspect, but that did not mean I had forgotten Nicholas Whitlock's motives. The less he knew about my investigation, the better.

"The police seem perfectly qualified to resolve this matter. I'm sure they do not need my help," I said. "In the last murder case you mentioned, the police were not investigating at all, which is why I was forced to become involved."

Nicholas nodded, but I could tell by the slight turning up of his mouth that he did not believe me. "Well, then your reasons are a mystery to me," he admitted. "As for me, I came here to search for more of my grandmother's belongings. Or for some kind of evidence that would connect Miss Brown to the crime."

"You believe she may have been involved?" I asked.

"My grandmother is the reason she lost her position, which seems like a motive for murder. Not for a sane mind, of course," he said. "But to the deranged, any slight is enough to turn them violent."

"True," I agreed. "Though, I hardly thought Miss Brown was deranged. She was a loyal servant to my aunt for the last year. It is hard to imagine her capable of such a thing."

"Stranger things have happened," he said with a wink. But before I could respond, Nicholas moved to the window and drew the curtain, cloaking the room in darkness. When he turned back to me, he was half-hidden in shadow. "You claim you are not investigating the murder, and perhaps you truly are not, but I hope I can persuade you otherwise."

My heart was thundering in my chest. The room was too small and too dark and too isolated. I felt as though I was suffocating. "You want me to investigate the murder?"

"You've done it before," he said. "Several times, if the other guests are to be believed. I do not know the police, but I know you, Rose. Well enough, at least. I've seen enough of you to know that you are an honest woman, and I would feel better knowing you had a hand in capturing my grandmother's killer."

"That is very kind of you to say, Nicholas."

"I meant every word," he said, crossing the room in three long strides and laying his hand on my shoulder. It all happened so quickly that I could not run away or keep my distance. My stomach tangled into knots as I looked up into his face, realizing how helpless I was in that moment to defend myself against him should he wish to hurt me. "I would really like for you to help me catch Miss Brown."

I smiled up at him, my lips trembling with nerves, and then slowly side-stepped his hand and moved around him towards the door. Nicholas made no move to stop me, but I was still much too aware of his presence behind me and how easy it would be for him to rush forward and block the door—my only escape. When I reached the door, I turned the handle and stepped halfway through it. A draft from the hallway ruffled my skirts, and I felt like I could breathe normally again. I would get out.

"If it would help ease your suffering, then I will keep

my eyes and ears open over the next few days for any signs of who could be responsible," I said. "I will do my best to catch *whoever* is guilty."

Nicholas beamed at me, his teeth reflecting light even in the dim room. "Thank you, Rose. I truly appreciate it."

I did not want to leave him alone in Miss Brown's room, but I also could not force myself to remain in the enclosed space with him for another moment. So, I nodded, stepped into the hallway, and hurried back up to my room where Alice was still sleeping.

15

Despite the excitement of the morning, the rest of the day passed slowly. Nicholas remained inside, not yet ready to face the entire party of guests, and Catherine and Charles too remained busy prepping for the wedding they desperately hoped would still happen. After breakfast, Charles and Vivian Barry moved out onto the grass—the first guests willing to do so since Aunt Augusta's death—and the rest of the table soon followed after.

Aunt Ruth and her three daughters had been angry and sullen ever since their attempt to move from Ridgewick Hall to the Inn had been foiled, but even they could not resist the allure of the warm sunshine and the soft breeze moving through the trees. Sitting out on the lawn, the sound of bird calls and swaying grasses filling the air, it was hard to remember the chaos of the garden party. The screams and cries for help as Dr. Shaw worked on Augusta Whitlock. That memory seemed too dark and distant for such a beautiful day.

Alice stayed close to me, watching me slightly more carefully than she ever had before, but doing nothing else to suggest the secret she had learned about my identity. When she wasn't observing me, she was running into the house to see if Nicholas needed anything. Vivian Barry had been doing her best to cater to Nicholas' needs during his time of mourning, and Alice seemed determined to out-do her. She found some reason or another to knock on his door three different times between breakfast and lunch and wrapped up a scone from the afternoon tea tray in a napkin to take to him since he did not come down for lunch.

Part of me wanted to know what Nicholas was doing alone in his room, but another part of me wanted nothing to do with him. Guilty of the murder or not, he made me uncomfortable, and I was happy to not have to be near him. I wanted to warn Alice away from him, but I knew it would be pointless. Not only would she not listen to me, but my warning her away would likely only increase her affections for the man even more. Lady Ashton whispered to her daughter multiple times that he was her cousin, and Alice insisted her interest in him was familial, but everyone could see through that. She had an infatuation that I hoped would end as soon as everyone returned to their normal lives and he was not within walking distance anymore.

Anytime Lady Ashton went back into the house to check on Catherine or talk with Lord Ashton, the guests began whispering about Augusta Whitlock's death. They did their best to be respectful around Catherine and Lady

Ashton, but they were understandably consumed with curiosity about the events surrounding it.

"I can't believe they really think it could be a murder," Aunt Ruth said to one of her daughters, though she said it loud enough for everyone in the grass to hear. "The woman was elderly. It seems obvious to me that she died of old age."

Lady Harwood harrumphed in disagreement. "She stumbled about the garden as though the ground was falling out from beneath her. I don't remember her doing that the first day she arrived. In my opinion, the illness came upon her suddenly."

"Illness?" one of the Blake daughters, who I suspected might have been Margaret, asked. She curled her legs underneath her on the grass, adjusting her pale blue dress over her knees, and turned to her mother, concerned. "No one mentioned anything about an illness."

"Because she was not ill," Aunt Ruth said. "She was old."

Lady Harwood turned her body away from Aunt Ruth as though she would not deign to speak to her, and instead spoke to the air, he voice carrying across the grass. "Everyone will see the truth when we all contract the same illness. Locked in this house as we are, like wild animals in a cage. It will not be long before we all begin to exhibit symptoms."

One of the maids carrying an empty glass into the house coughed to clear her throat, and Lady Harwood lifted a finger in the air, eyes wide. "You see? No, it will not be long now."

Dr. Shaw sat in a chair near Lady Harwood doing his best to ignore her. He had taken her temperature too many times to count and could do nothing further to reassure her she was not dying, so he stayed quiet.

Aunt Ruth and Lady Harwood continued their debate, each of them pretending they were not talking to one another, though they responded to each other's theories, and I adjusted my position in the grass. My hands were beginning to tingle from holding them behind me to prop myself up. However, when I sat up straight and folded my hands in my lap, they continued to tingle. Soon, the tingling became a constant burn. As though my fingers were positioned ever so slightly too close to a raging fire. I stared down at my hands, turning them over in my lap, studying my skin. Was it just too much sun or were they beginning to turn red?

"Rose?" Alice asked, leaning in. "Are you all right?"

"Yes, fine," I said, tucking my hands in a fold of my dress.

She nodded and went back to relaxing on the grass, but I could feel her eyes on me. I tried to ignore the pain in my skin, but the longer I sat there, the worse the sensation became. Finally, I excused myself and hurried up towards the house. Once inside, I went straight into the washroom.

My hands were red and tender, small bumps covering my skin from wrists to fingertips. I turned on the faucet and ran my hands under the cool water, feeling momentary relief.

What was happening? A reaction to the grass or the heat, perhaps? I'd never had any issues before, but it was all I could think of. Besides that, the itching feeling seemed to invade my mind and wipe away thoughts of anything else.

After washing my hands several times and gingerly patting them dry, I walked back outside and caught Dr. Shaw's attention. Lady Harwood narrowed her eyes at me, bothered that I would disturb her personal physician, but Dr. Shaw pushed himself to standing and followed me beneath the shade of a large tree, anyway. I could feel Alice's eyes on me the entire time.

"Is something the matter?" he asked.

"I'm not sure," I said honestly, pulling my hands from behind my back. "I'm sorry to bother you, but I think I may be having a reaction to something. I'm not sure what."

Dr. Shaw blinked and then leaned closer, widening his eyes as if to see better. "When did this appear?"

"Just now. While we were out in the grass." Dr. Shaw was tilting his head from one side to the other and furrowing his brow. I'd never seen him so animated before. My heart began to race. "Do you know what it is?"

Suddenly, Dr. Shaw grabbed my elbow and pulled me closer to the house, safely out of earshot of the other guests. He stopped in a thin strip of shade that ran along the back of the house. It would disappear as the sun rose higher in the sky, but it was cool and damp while we stood there.

"Just this morning I was consulted by the local coroner to examine Augusta Whitlock's body," Dr. Shaw said, his voice low and urgent.

"I thought you'd already examined her?"

He shook his head. "I checked her pulse and her vitals. I observed her body for any obvious signs of trauma, but I did not look beyond the layers of her clothing. That was for the coroner here to do, but when he did, he found something concerning."

A cool dread slipped down my spine, goosebumps creeping outward from the center of my back. "What did he find?"

Dr. Shaw tipped his head down, his eyes moving to my hands. "A rash very similar to the one on your hands."

I stuck out my hand to catch myself on the stone wall. The brush of the stone against my fingertips stung, and I hissed.

"But worse," Dr. Shaw added quickly. "Much worse. This rash covered her entire body. From neck to ankle and shoulder to wrist. She was covered in red, angry welts. Neither of us could make sense of what it was. I still don't know. The only thing I do know is that it is no coincidence you have the same rash."

I shook my head, trying to make sense of everything. Aunt Augusta wore thick velvet clothing that covered every inch of her body. Like me, she could have been suffering from some sort of adverse reaction to the heat. Or something in the grass.

Or, I could be the next target of the killer. My heart leapt in my chest, and I took a deep breath to calm myself.

"Did she have the rash on her hands?" I asked. "Or her face?"

Dr. Shaw shook his head. "It stopped at her wrists

and her ankles and the base of her neck. It was only where her clothes touched her skin."

My forehead wrinkled as I tried to put together the puzzle pieces forming in my mind. They fit together, I just had to figure out how.

Aunt Augusta's rash was only under her clothing, while mine was on my hands. It meant that we had not come into contact with the irritant in the same way, which suggested I was not under attack but had simply come into contact with the poison by accident.

Suddenly, I remembered the powder on the floor of Miss Brown's closet. I'd massaged it into my fingers and both of my hands had touched the floor of her closet. It would explain why I only had the rash on my hands. But how had it appeared in the closet in the first place?

"It was almost as though her own dress had poisoned her," Dr. Shaw said, shaking his head. "It was the strangest thing I've ever seen."

I could see Miss Brown's closet in my mind. Except, this time, her things were still in the room. Her Bible was on the nightstand and her three simple dresses were hanging on the right side of the closet. And on the right... one of Aunt Augusta's gowns.

When questioned, Miss Brown claimed the dress had mud on the hem and she'd simply brought it to her room to clean it. I could see Nicholas pulling it from the closet directly above where I'd seen the powder.

The only way for Aunt Augusta to be covered in the rash would be for her entire body to have been coated in it. Which it was. Because the poison had been on the inside of her gown.

The same gown Aunt Augusta wore to the garden party the day she died.

The puzzle pieces in my mind locked into place, and I could finally see the answer.

Miss Brown killed Augusta Whitlock.

16

I couldn't remember saying goodbye to Dr. Shaw. I wasn't sure that I said anything to him at all. As soon as the reality settled over me, I ran into the house to find George. He wasn't in the kitchen talking with the staff or in his room in the servant quarters, so I walked through a side entrance and out towards the garage. The large wooden doors were thrown open, and I could see George inside cleaning the car.

When I called his name, he stood up, his head popping up from behind the car, and held a hand to his forehead, squinting into the sun.

"Miss Beckingham?"

George knew me well enough to call me Rose. He had worked for me, but he had also saved my life. We had been on adventures together, and yet he insisted on the formality. It was a comfort I would not deprive him of.

"Yes. George. Hello," I said, out of breath. My hands were still aching, but it was a dull pain, easily pushed aside in favor of the excitement I now felt. "I wanted to ask you a few questions."

He came around to the front of the car and leaned against the shiny hood. "All right. What about?"

"Miss Brown."

He frowned. "I told the police all I know. I wish I knew more. She looked suspicious when I saw her here the day of the garden party, but I really don't know anything else."

"But you saw her here that day?" I asked. "The day after she was dismissed from her duties?"

He nodded. "I did."

"She didn't stay at Ridgewick that night, so if she was here the next day, then she had to have stayed somewhere close by."

"I thought of that, too," he said, taking off his driver's cap and running a hand through his gray hair. "Before we came to Ridgewick, I spoke with Miss Brown. She was excited about the trip because of Miss Catherine's wedding, of course, but also because Miss Brown's sister lived in the near village. She was looking forward to visiting her, so I would bet she is staying there."

"Did she mention her sister's name?" I asked excitedly.

George screwed up his mouth to one side in thought and then shook his head. "I don't believe she did. I'm sorry."

"That's all right. I'm sure I can still find her."

George frowned. "You won't be able to leave the property, Miss. Not with the police officers on watch."

I'd forgotten about the guard entirely. That was yet another hurdle I would need to face.

"Oh, of course. I forgot about that. Oh well," I said, acting as though it didn't really matter. "Thank you for your help, George."

"Not sure how much help it was," he said, shrugging and going back to cleaning the car. "But I'm happy to have done it."

THE TABLE WAS BEING SET for dinner when I made it back inside. Catherine and Charles were huddled together in the sitting room while Charles Barry eyed them from where he was leaning against the dining room door, waiting for the kitchen staff to finish readying the table. Alice was talking with Nicholas, who had finally found his way downstairs for a meal, and Lady Ashton was whispering with Lord Ashton in the corner. If there wasn't so much on my mind, I would have been worried about Lord and Lady Ashton. Ever since they arrived in Ridgewick, Lord Ashton had been withdrawn and quiet. He hadn't seemed interested in anything, and he hardly paid attention to Lady Ashton. I knew it was because being in Ridgewick Hall reminded him of their last trip here with Edward and everything that had happened afterward. But there was too much I needed to do to worry about that now.

"How are you this evening?" Dr. Shaw asked, shuffling over to stand next to me. He glanced down at my hands, and I folded them behind my back.

"Well, thank you," I said, not feeling well at all. I needed to get out of the house. I needed to get past the officers and into the village. I needed to see Miss Brown.

The household staff finished setting the table and walked briskly back into the kitchen. The guests descended on the table, but I held back. Once everyone was seated, Lady Ashton looked over at me, beckoning me towards the table, but I took a step backwards and shook my head.

"Actually, I'm really not feeling well," I said.

Lady Ashton frowned and made to stand up, but I waved her away. "I'm fine. Really. I think I will just forego dinner and go lie down instead."

Before anyone could argue, I left the room and slowly walked up the stairs.

From the window in my room, I could see the officers standing watch at the doors. Even if I crawled out my window, they would see me. I needed to somehow draw them away from the doors long enough for me to escape. I was standing at the window, staring down at the top of the officer's heads, when the door creaked open. I turned to see Alice slipping inside.

"Is everything all right?" she asked quietly. "I came to check on you. Nicholas was very impressed with my thoughtfulness."

I resisted the urge to roll my eyes and got to the point. "I need to leave the house. Tonight."

"Leave?" Alice asked, forehead wrinkled. "You can't leave. I told you, Rose, I'll stand behind you when you tell Mama and Papa about your identity and—"

"I plan to return," I amended. "I just need to get into the village to talk to someone."

I expected a rush of questions and for Alice to beg to accompany me, but instead, she simply nodded once and lifted her chin, looking much more mature than I'd ever seen her. "What do you need me to do?"

I looked back out the window and then shrugged. "I need a distraction. Something that will pull the guards from the door."

She took a step forward and leaned through the window to see the officers. Then, she stood tall, placed her hands on her hips, and walked back towards the door. When she turned back to me, there was a mischievous smile on her face. "Run when you hear the screaming."

Before I could ask what she meant, she was gone.

I followed after Alice several seconds later, but she was already moving down the stairs. From the second floor landing, I could see her walk through the entrance hall towards the dining room. Someone—Lady Ashton, I presumed—asked her if I was all right. Alice began to answer, but halfway through the words, her voice cut out. Then, there was a thud. And then a scream.

"Alice?" Lady Ashton cried.

Chair legs scraped against the wooden floor and people gasped.

"She fainted," Catherine said.

Lady Harwood called for Dr. Shaw and Lord Ashton bellowed something to the servants about water and towels.

Then, just as I'd hoped, the officers standing guard

opened the front door, and upon seeing the commotions, abandoned their posts and ran inside. As soon as they were in the dining room, I ran down the stairs, through the front door, and down the center pathway that led to the road.

I'D NEVER BEEN in the village before. It was quaint with stone streets and sidewalks built into the hillside. Bakeries, shops, and schools dotted the roads, closed in by wrought iron gates. Lights and fires blazed behind windows and laughter floated out of the local inn as I passed.

The only tip I had to go on was Miss Brown's surname. It was a common name, so I did not have much hope at all as I opened the door to the local pub and walked up to the bartender. He was wiping out the inside of a glass with a rag. His head was bald, covered by a hat that looked to be several sizes too small, and he smelled of liquor and smoke. Still, when he looked up, he gave me a gruff smile.

"Can I help you?" he growled.

"Actually, yes," I said as politely as I could. "I'm looking for someone, but I'm afraid I do not have much information to go on."

He placed the glass on a shelf behind him rim down and then turned back to me, threw the towel over his shoulder, and crossed his arms. "You came to the right place. I know everyone in this town. My family has owned the pub for fifty years. I've grown up here."

"Wonderful," I said, truly meaning it. "I'm looking for a Miss Brown. The woman I'm looking for is new in town —mousy brown hair, medium-height. I believe she is staying with her sister who lives in the village. I'm not sure of her name, so—"

"It is Brown, too," he said, cutting me off. "The new woman came into the pub with her sister just the other day. She didn't look well. Crying and moaning about losing work. I gave her a drink on the house."

"Do you know where I can find her?" I asked.

My excitement was clearly more than the man was accustomed to, and he pulled back, eyebrows pinched together. "Are you a friend?"

"An acquaintance," I admitted. "Though, I do not mean them any harm."

This seemed an appropriate enough response for the man because he directed me to the end of the block and two streets over. "A small cottage with a wooden bucket of flowers on the front porch. You can't miss it."

He was right. I couldn't. The cottage was small, but well-kept. Prior to living with the Beckinghams in India and then in London, I would have called it an oasis. It was far nicer than the New York City apartment where I'd grown up.

There was a light shining through a heavy curtain over the front window, and I stood outside on the sidewalk for a moment, trying to wait for any sign of movement. There was none. Finally, I crossed the narrow street, mounted the two steps to the front door, and knocked.

My hands, still burning slightly from the contact I'd

had with the poison earlier, trembled at my sides. I did not know what I would say to Miss Brown. I could not confront her with the accusation of murder because I had no proof. If I let her know I suspected her, she could run, and justice would never be served. Really, I just came for more evidence. For some sense of a motive for the crime. I didn't know Miss Brown well, but from what I did know about her, she was a kind, helpful woman. She did her best to make life easier for those around her and did so with a smile. So, could Augusta Whitlock really have bothered her enough in one day to lead her to murder?

The door opened and a woman who looked remarkably like Miss Brown stood in the doorway. She had on a simple dark dress that hung past her knees and a sweater over the top. Her brown hair was twisted into a bun at the base of her neck.

"Yes?" she said in lieu of a greeting.

"Hello, I'm looking for...Miss Brown," I said, realizing at once I had no idea what Miss Brown's first name was. "I believe she is your sister."

She glanced back over her shoulder, and then turned back to me. "And who should I say is here?"

"Rose Beckingham." I almost extended my hand but quickly thought better of it. Evening was coming on quickly, but there was still enough light to see the rash across my fingers and the palms of my hands.

Miss Brown's sister nodded, disappeared inside for a few seconds, and then returned and pulled the door wide. "Come on in, Miss Beckingham. I'm Emma Brown."

The house was even smaller inside than it looked from the outside, but it was bright and cozy. The fire in the hearth filled the room with a warmth that was almost overwhelming, and directly in front of the fire was Miss Brown.

I nearly gasped when I saw her.

She had always been plain looking, but lying on the sofa in front of the fire wrapped in a blanket as she was, she looked ill. Her skin was pale and her brown hair hung around her face in limp strands. And despite the warmth of the room, she seemed to be shivering.

Despite my suspicions about her, I drew near and knelt next to the sofa. "Miss Brown. What happened to you?"

She turned to me, her lips chapped and cracking. "Call me Rebecca, please."

"Rebecca, what happened?"

Miss Brown lifted herself out of her cocoon of blankets and propped herself up. As she did, her hands came out from under the blankets, and I saw the blue tint to her fingertips. "I'm not sure. A few days ago, I became suddenly ill."

"After you left Ridgewick Hall?" I asked.

She nodded. "The very day. I came to my sister's house to figure out what to do next and a rash began to form on my arms and my hands and my neck. It became worse and worse. I wanted to go back to the house to apologize to everyone and beg for my job back, but the rash was overwhelming. I had to be seen by a doctor."

I glanced down at my hands and wondered how much worse my own rash would become. Would it spread? I tried my best to push the thought from my mind.

"The next day, the rash had subsided, and I felt good enough to walk back to Ridgewick Hall," she said, her voice growing faint with every word as though it took a great deal of energy for her to speak with me. "I arrived in the afternoon and planned to find Lady Ashton, but from the dining room, I saw Augusta Whitlock fall. I heard everyone scream, and I became frightened. I had threatened her before I'd left, and I worried what would happen if anyone knew I'd come back, so I grabbed a few things from my room and ran."

I studied Rebecca's face, trying to determine how much of what she was telling me was the truth, but it was impossible to say. She was weak and her usual demeanor was lost beneath a haze of illness.

"If you became well enough to walk to Ridgewick, how did you end up like this?" I asked.

Miss Brown shook her head. "I do not know. Once I returned home, the symptoms came over me slowly. First, there was dizziness. And then fevers and shakes. The village doctor has been stopping in to see me, but even he is perplexed by what has come over me. The only hope we have is that I appear to be getting better."

My eyes widened at that remark. If this was Miss Brown feeling better, then what had she looked like in the worst of it?

I could hear Emma Brown moving around in the small kitchen behind me. Moments later, she walked around the small sofa holding a cup of broth. She helped her sister sit up taller and began to feed her.

"Would you like anything, Miss Beckingham?" Emma asked. "Tea or broth?"

I declined. "I should be leaving soon."

Rebecca turned to me, her tired eyes curious. "Why did you come all this way? How did you know I was here?"

"I came to ensure you were all right," I said. "And to tell you that your position within the Beckingham household will be there for you once you are well again."

Hope sparked behind her eyes, giving her a sense of life I hadn't seen in her since I'd arrived. "Are you telling the truth?"

"I am," I said. "Lady Ashton has missed you, and I know we can explain to her that this was all a misunderstanding."

Rebecca Brown practically sagged in relief. "Thank heavens. Because I did not steal that necklace. I would never steal from anyone. I have no idea how it came to be in my room."

Emma pressed a hand to her sister's shoulder, trying to keep her from getting too excited, and I stood up, realizing it was time to excuse myself. "I know, Rebecca. I'm positive we will know all of the answers soon enough. You get well, and I will see you again soon."

The sisters smiled and waved as I left. I paused outside of their house for just a moment, taking in the quiet street around me. And then I ran.

I ran as fast as I could, my arms pumping at my sides. I ran until my lungs were heaving and I thought I would faint. I had to get back to Ridgewick Hall as quickly as I could. I needed to warn everyone.

There was a killer living amongst them.

17

Lights flared from Ridgewick Hall as though each window was an eye staring down at me as I ran up the long road that led to the house. Once I reached the wide, shallow steps just inside the gate, I slowed down, allowing my breathing to calm. If I ran into the officers standing guard, I didn't want them to see me looking tired or alarmed. My only plan for getting past them without raising suspicion was to act as though nothing was wrong and inform them I had been on a long walk.

As it turned out, that was unnecessary. The front door was unmanned.

I pushed it open, stepped into the entrance hall, and closed it quietly behind me. The dining room straight ahead was empty and so was the sitting room to the left. When I reached the wide open double doors that led into the dining room, I saw movement on the terrace.

Lady Harwood was in her wheelchair near the doors with Dr. Shaw sitting close by, but the rest of the party was out on the grass. Catherine and Charles were as inseparable as ever, sitting together on a small grassy hill a short distance from where Aunt Ruth was watching her silly adult daughters laugh and giggle to themselves like small children. Alice was sitting at the base of a large tree with her entire attention turned towards Nicholas, who was pointing out something in the night sky. Vivian was on Nicholas' other side with Charles Barry next to her, his shoulders stooped forward in frustration—his permanent attitude since Catherine had made it clear she had no intention of calling off her wedding. Even Lord Ashton, who had resisted mingling too much with the guests during our week at Ridgewick Hall, was standing in the back garden with his arm around Lady Ashton's waist.

The guards were standing just outside the terrace doors, overseeing the group, and I wondered whether it wasn't Alice's doing. Whether she hadn't convinced everyone to sit outside to allow me to sneak back into the house. If it was, I had no intention of misusing the gift. I turned around and went up the stairs at once, heading straight for the room at the opposite end of the hall from my own.

My heart thundered in my chest as I pushed open the door, even though I had just seen all of the house's occupants sitting outside in the grass. I knew no one would be inside. Still, I opened the door slowly and slipped in when it was only opened a crack, doing my best to walk across the hardwood floor as quietly as possible.

The room was dark, but there was enough light coming from the moon through the curtains for me to see that Nicholas Whitlock's room was a mess. The bed was unmade, his clothes were scattered across the floor and the dresser as though he was using them as drop cloths, and papers covered the desk and table next to his bed. Clearly, he had not allowed a maid into the room since he had arrived, and now I knew why.

Nicholas Whitlock had killed his grandmother.

The moment I saw Rebecca Brown's blue fingertips, I knew the truth. She, like myself, had come into contact with the poison through Aunt Augusta's dress. The dress that Nicholas removed from Miss Brown's closet, leaving a dusting of poison on the floor. The dress he helped his grandmother change into for the garden party. The dress she died in.

I knew this to be true, but it wasn't enough to have him arrested. The facts could easily be spun to point the finger at Miss Brown, who I knew without a doubt was innocent. I needed to find the poison in Nicholas' belongings or something that would cement his involvement or make clear his motive. Augusta Whitlock's secret will would be a wonderful piece of evidence.

I picked through the mess carefully, not wanting another run in with the poison. If Miss Brown's symptoms were any indication, I would be ill for several more days, and I did not want another dosage to make things worse. So, I slipped my hand into the pockets of his trousers slowly and ran my fingers along the insides of his jackets. Once I finished with an item, I did my best to replace it in the same condition I'd found it, though that made it difficult to see where I'd been. The space was such a mess that my best option was to move in a counterclockwise fashion around the room. So, that was what I did.

I checked the drawers of his dresser and the clothes there before moving to the closet where I searched the few items that were still hanging up. When I finally worked my way to the desk in front of the window, I ducked down to be sure I stayed out of view of the guests out on the back lawn, though I checked once to be sure everyone was still outside.

The desk was littered with correspondence that proved to be nothing more than useless gossip and friendly conversation between Nicholas and his friends. After some time, I began to skim through the pages, hoping for something to jump out at me. That was when I came across what looked to be a receipt. Except, it was not for money spent, but money paid. On the ledger it described a silver goblet and a painting that someone sold to an auction house in London for a hefty sum. Suddenly, I remembered Aunt Augusta complaining about her home in London being robbed. She said the thieves stole silver from her dining room and a painting from the attic. Nicholas had insisted the items were just misplaced, but then, of course he would. He had been the one to steal them, after all.

I found more receipts for other items I could only assume did not belong to Nicholas—dresses, shoes, handbags, and hats, as well as jewelry and more paintings. He had been stealing from his grandmother for some time and selling the items to keep the money himself. But apparently, that venture was no longer as lucrative as Nicholas desired. Killing his grandmother and inheriting her fortune would net a far larger sum. One he did not have to lie and steal for. If only he had her secret will.

No sooner had the thought crossed my mind than I turned over a paper on the desk and saw a handwritten note in loopy, trembling cursive. The letter was written in Aunt Augusta's shaky hand, and in it, she surrendered all of her worldly possessions to her "dearest grandson Nicholas Whitlock" should she die. It was dated six months earlier.

He'd found it. Nicholas had the secret will, so all that was left to do was get rid of his grandmother and he could have the life of lavish luxury he'd always wanted. So, he did.

Excitement and fear rushed through me as I folded the will with shaking hands, still itching from the powdered poison I'd encountered that morning, and tucked it beneath the collar of my dress.

"It's not right to take what isn't yours."

The voice startled me, and I let out a yelp as I spun around, knocking into the desk and sending a stack of papers scattering across the floor.

Nicholas looked down at the new mess and shook his head. "You have made such a mess, Rose."

"I didn't hear you come in," I said, trying to stay calm. "I wasn't stealing from you. I was just—"

"Solving my grandmother's murder?" He tilted his head to the side, eyebrows pinched together in concern. He shut the door behind him, pinning us into the room. It suddenly felt warmer and stuffier, as though all of the air was shut out on the other side. "I saw you sneak away from the house earlier. Alice's distraction fooled everyone else, but it did not fool me."

"I went for a long walk," I said, using the same lie I'd planned to tell the guards. "I needed the fresh air."

Nicholas shook his head, not believing anything I was saying, and continued on. "I knew you were getting close to the truth. It is why you and I kept running into one another. You were following all of the right clues, and if I hadn't been so annoyed, I would have been impressed."

"I don't know what you're talking about," I lied. "You are frightening me."

Nicholas smiled, his lips curling up at the corners, but the smile was not at all friendly. It was the snarl of a wolf before it rips into its prey. It was deadly. "If you are hoping to appeal to my sense of mercy, Rose, you will find I do not have one. Besides, I know you are much cleverer than you let on. For instance, you know the truth about me."

"What truth?" I asked, raising my chin, doing my best not to let him see it trembling in fear. I could still hear the guests outside on the grass. Their voices were distant, and I knew even if they heard my screams, they would not find me soon enough. Nicholas was standing between me and the exit, and the only way out would be to fight.

Nicholas took a step towards me, and I pressed my legs even harder against the edge of the desk, desperate for more space between us. He leaned forward, his eyes shining with a kind of amusement I'd never seen before. "I'm a murderer."

"Why?" I asked, dropping the façade of ignorance. "Was it only for the money?"

"You make it sound as though that is not a good enough reason," he said. "Though, of course you would say that. You have always had money. You have no idea what it is like to live without it. Besides that, your family is dead. You are a wealthy, single woman."

"You do not know anything about me," I said.

He rolled his eyes and continued. "My entire plan was quite genius, I think. I knew it would look suspicious if Augusta died too soon after her grandson came to care for her. There would be so many questions and concerned relatives looking for their cut of the inheritance. So, rather than poisoning her in one dose, I poisoned her slowly over the course of a year, giving her just enough to make her ill, to make her dependent upon me. Without the poison, she was an independent old woman without need of anyone. With it, however, she needed a steady hand to help her down the stairs and to the dining room. She needed someone to make her meals and keep her house in order, and I filled that role."

"She trusted you," I said, eyes narrowed, unsure how I hadn't seen from the beginning what a cold-hearted monster Nicholas was. "She left her inheritance to her 'dearest grandson,' and you betrayed her. You murdered her."

He shook his head. "Do not pretend you cared for the old woman. You are not even related to her. Or me, for that matter. Even if you had been, it would not have changed the fact that Augusta Whitlock was a miserable old woman who made those around her miserable, as well. No one will miss her. She had so much money but refused to share it. She kept it to herself and would only give it to her family if they agreed to wait on her like servants while she was alive. She was selfish and cruel. I simply took what was mine."

I felt sick. Actually nauseous. How could anyone be so heartless? I pushed down my rising nausea and tried to focus on how I would escape the room.

"Why here?" I asked. "Why this weekend?"

"Ah," he said, lifting his finger in the air. "Another genius idea of mine. I wanted her to die in a public place. A place where there would be witnesses, people to attest to how devotedly I cared for her. I did not want her to die at home where no one would see it and people could suspect. So, just before we left for the wedding, I increased her dosage of the poison. Then, once here, I coated the inside of her clothing with it. She had grown accustomed to the burning and the itching, thinking it a symptom of her ageing body, but the dizziness worsened. She became unsteady and feverish. I knew her death would come quickly, and that it did. The heat of the garden party must have made the poison work more quickly. Even I was surprised when she fell so suddenly."

"Can you really be such a genius if the police have launched an investigation?" I asked.

His smile hardened around the edges, his eyes narrowing further into slits. "You are the only one who suspects me, Rose. The only person who stands in the way of me inheriting what is rightfully mine."

I slid away from the desk and pressed my back against the wall. When I turned my head, I could see movement on the garden below through a sliver in the curtain. I was so close to safety, yet so far. I could not jump from the window without dying or scream without Nicholas attacking. I was trapped with nowhere else to turn.

"They will know it was you if you kill me," I said. "You are the only one inside the house. If I turn up dead, they will suspect."

He shook his head. "You forget, Rose. Everyone thinks you went to bed hours ago because you were not feeling well. Would it be such a surprise if you suddenly died? Would it be impossible for you to have been sicker than you let on? Whereas, I only came inside for ten, fifteen minutes at the most. Just long enough to grab my hat and a book to read to Alice on the lawn. She is really quite infatuated with me, isn't she? Even your beloved cousin would not suspect I could be such a monster." He took a step closer to me, his entire body poised and ready for a fight, prepared to dart out and stop me should I try to run in either direction. "I will leave this house and your death will be a tragedy. Perhaps, I'll even attend your funeral. Do not worry, I'll tell everyone of your kindness and intelligence. I will offer a touching tribute."

He took another step towards me, and I knew the time for conversation was over. If I did not get out now, I would never escape. I lunged to the right and ducked, hoping to run under his arm, but Nicholas kicked out his leg, striking me in the chest. The blow knocked the wind out of me, and I stumbled back, hitting the desk once again. The edge of the wood pinched my spine, and I cried out in pain.

"Do not make this worse than it needs to be, Rose," Nicholas said calmly, though his breathing was heavier than before. I looked up just in time to see him pull something small from the inside of his jacket pocket. I heard the pop of pressure as he uncorked it. "Take a deep breath and the poison should work quickly."

Suddenly, he flicked his wrist, and the same white, shimmery powder I'd found in Miss Brown's closet was in the air. I threw myself backwards, sliding across the cluttered floor, and closed my eyes, desperate to keep the poison from touching me.

"I have worked up quite the immunity," Nicholas said, looking unfazed as he skirted the edge of the dust cloud. "You, unfortunately, will be overcome quickly. Even that small amount in the servant's closet was enough to make you ill. This amount will have you unconscious within the minute. Alice will be so distraught when she finds you in her bed this evening. Do not worry, I will comfort her."

Nicholas' hand wrapped around my wrist, and I kicked out at him, pushing against the floor to avoid the cloud of poison. If I breathed it in, I would be dead. I pulled on my arm, trying to free it from his grip, but he was too strong. I squeezed my eyes shut, turned my head, and held my breath as he began to drag me across the floor.

Then, suddenly, his hand fell away from my wrist and there was a loud thud.

I stilled for a moment, nervous to open my eyes or move for fear of the poison. Then, another hand wrapped around my wrist. This one smaller and gentler.

"Rose?"

My eyes flew open. Alice was standing in front of me, Nicholas' hunting rifle held in her other hand. The handle of it was covered in blood. My eyes moved from the gun to the lump of shadow on the floor—Nicholas. He was unconscious, a puddle of blood forming under his head.

"He is unconscious, but we have to go," Alice said. "Now."

I did not hesitate as I grabbed my youngest cousin's hand and allowed her to lead me out of the room—avoiding the worst of the poison cloud—and into the hallway. I did not let go of her hand even as we ran onto the terrace and told the police standing guard everything. I clung to her as though if I let go, I would float away. And I thought I could feel Alice holding onto me with the same ferocity.

18

Alice had overheard much of my conversation with Nicholas. She'd come up to the house to check on him a few minutes after he'd gone inside, and I would be forever grateful that she had. Without her testimony of the event, there may have been a lot more doubt of my version. She was able to tell the two officers at the house—and their sergeant when he arrived within the hour—that Nicholas had planned and executed the murder of his grandmother and had planned the same for me. I stood by her as she was interrogated, squeezing her hand as she ensured the imprisonment of the man she had been infatuated with.

Though, later, once the interrogation was over, Alice insisted she had never much cared for Nicholas.

"He wept so much when his grandmother died," she said, wrinkling her nose in distaste. "It was a bit too much. I could never be with a man who was so emotional."

"You didn't seem to mind a few days ago," Catherine

said, smiling for the first time since we'd arrived at Ridgewick. Her wedding would go on as scheduled, and I didn't think anything in the world could have brought her down.

Alice glared at her sister and then sank back into the cushions of the sofa. "I know I should go to bed, but I'm not tired in the least."

"Neither am I," I admitted.

The rest of the guests in the house—everyone aside for myself, Alice, Catherine, and Lord and Lady Ashton —had gone to bed as soon as the excitement of Nicholas' arrest had begun to wane. Lady Ashton had to dissuade Aunt Ruth from leaving with her daughters to stay at the Inn at once.

"You only have one more night before the wedding," she said, laying a comforting hand on her sister-in-law's back and leading her towards the stairs. "The killer has been caught, so there is nothing to worry about. You can leave tomorrow. Please, stay with us."

"I couldn't care less where she stays either way," Lord Ashton whispered to Catherine, who laughed.

It was nice to see the family relaxed for once. The weeks leading up to the wedding had been stressful for everyone, and Aunt Augusta's death had done little to ease everyone's nerves. Now, however, that the case had been solved, it seemed as though everyone could finally take a breath at last.

Except for me.

With the mystery solved and the family quickly settling back into their normal rhythms, I couldn't help but wonder what my place in their lives would look like moving forward. Alice knew the truth about my identity and had still chosen to attack Nicholas and save my life, so I knew she was on my side. But what would happen when Catherine and Lady Ashton uncovered the truth? Or Lord Ashton, for that matter? I was a large reason why his son had gone to prison, which was where he was murdered. So, in his eyes, I could be the cause of his son's death. Would he still tolerate my presence in his household once he knew we were not related? Or, would they all feel foolish for having believed my lies? Would they kick me to the streets or call the police to report me for theft? Rose's inheritance did not belong to me, after all. In a way, I was no better than Nicholas Whitlock. I had not killed Rose and her family for my inheritance, but I had taken it all the same. Would they think me a criminal?

Lady Ashton came back into the room with a big sigh and sat down next to her husband, her hand affectionately on his knee. "This week has been even more exciting than I expected."

"Charles feels the same way," Catherine said. "By the time the police were carrying Nicholas out, he was already prepared to go upstairs and go straight to sleep. After nearly being killed in New York City and then living with a murderer here, he was feeling overwhelmed."

"I nearly forgot about that," Alice said with a laugh. "Funny how I could forget he was almost killed. Our lives are far too interesting, it seems, if something like that slips my mind."

Catherine nodded and then turned to me. "And if it had not been for Rose, Charles may have died. We wouldn't have been here this weekend at all. Though, according to Nicholas' own admission, his not coming to my wedding would not have saved Aunt Augusta. He would have killed her regardless."

"Still," Catherine continued, tipping her head down and looking up at me from beneath long lashes. "You saved his life, Rose, and now you've solved another murder. Perhaps, the Sergeant should offer you a position."

"I have had more than my fair share of excitement," I admitted, doing my best to smile.

Catherine frowned. "Is something the matter, Rose?"

"Yes," Alice said, squeezing my hand. "You've just saved the day. You should be ecstatic."

I looked down at my youngest cousin, and I could see the encouragement in her eyes. She wanted me to tell her family the truth. She wanted me to confess my true identity, and as much as I didn't want to do anything to ruin Catherine's wedding day, I wanted to confess, too. The secret seemed to weigh on me like an anchor around my feet, and I was ready to get rid of it.

I let go of Alice's hand, stood up, and walked to the front of the room, standing in front of the fireplace. Everyone's eyes followed me. Lady Ashton looked worried, her face pinched in concern. I took a deep breath and let it out in a long sigh. "Something is the matter."

"Tell us at once," Lady Ashton said, sounding urgent. "Please, Rose. We are family."

I smiled at her, wondering if she would feel the same way in another minute. "That is the problem," I said quietly, losing the nerve to maintain eye contact and looking down at my feet. "We are not family."

I heard the rustle of everyone shifting in their seats, leaning forward or away from me, trying to figure out what I meant.

"You all mean so much to me," I said, talking through a thick throat as tears brimmed in my eyes. "You have taken me in and treated me with more kindness than I ever could have hoped for, and I love each of you so dearly, but we are not family. I...am not Rose Beckingham."

There was a long silence, and I finally found the courage to look up. Alice was giving me a sad smile, her big brown eyes warm and comforting. Catherine's mouth was hanging open, her forehead wrinkled in thought. Lord and Lady Ashton had mirrored faces of confusion. They needed to know more, and I was willing to tell them everything. The entire story.

So, I did.

I started with the murder of my parents and the disappearance of my brother. I told them about the orphanage I lived in while I was in New York City and about being assigned to work for the Beckinghams in India. I told them of my friendship with Rose and the wonderful years I spent with the family and how deeply I cared for them. Then, I talked about the bombing and how I was mistaken for Rose in the hospital. I explained that I had no one and nothing. That I would have been destitute on the streets of India with no way to return home.

"I know that is not an excuse," I said, tears beginning

to flow now. "And I know that the hope I gave you in thinking Rose had survived only to take it away now is beyond cruel, but I felt hopeless and helpless, and becoming Rose was my only chance at getting back to America and finding my brother. But then, you all were so lovely. You cared about Rose so much, and it became more difficult to leave. Eventually, I realized I didn't have any family left—not even my brother—and if I let you all go, too, I would have no one. So, I did not tell you the truth. I continued to lie, and I am forever sorry."

Shame washed over me in a wave, and I stood in front of them, shaking and waiting for a reply. I expected them to throw me from the house. To call the police back and have them arrest me at once. I expected every possibility except for the one that actually occurred.

"Sorry for what?" Lady Ashton asked, standing up and crossing the room to grab my hands. She lifted my chin with her finger and looked into my eyes. "Are you sorry for taking care of my girls as though they were your own sisters? Sorry for becoming a vital member of this family?"

I opened and closed my mouth, unsure what to say or how to respond.

Catherine stood up and moved to stand behind her mother, her hand on my shoulder. "Are you sorry for saving Charles' life? For making sure my wedding day wasn't ruined?"

"You have nothing to be sorry for," Alice said. She turned to her family. "I figured out the truth, and I don't love Rose any less for it. She is still family to me."

Lady Ashton and Catherine nodded, and I stared at

them with my mouth hanging open, unable to believe it. Unable to accept their kindness.

Then, Lady Ashton turned to her husband, and I realized there was one key voice that was missing. The vote that would determine whether I could remain or would be forced to leave. I followed her gaze to where Lord Ashton still sat on the couch, one leg crossed over the other, his forehead wrinkled in thought. As I looked at him, he turned and met my gaze. It felt like one of the first times he had looked at me—really looked at me—since I'd come to live with them almost a year before.

Then, his forehead smoothed and he shrugged. "We have lost too many people already to get rid of another member of the family. And that's what you are, Rose. You are a member of the family."

The tears began to flow freely, and Lady Ashton wrapped me in a hug. She smelled like lilies and cinnamon, and I breathed her in, grateful for their acceptance and love. "You are like a daughter to me, dear. Whether Rose Beckingham is your name or not, that will not change."

I sniffled. "I was Nellie Dennet. Before."

"And you can be Nellie Dennet again," Lady Ashton said. "If you want."

The decision felt too big and overwhelming, as I wavered back and forth, trying to decide who I was now. Who I had become.

"Do not feel you have to decide now," Catherine said. "Take your time."

With a squeal, Alice jumped up from the couch and

ran to join our group hug. "Yes. No matter what, you will always be the same person to me."

I hugged them all back and cried like I hadn't let myself cry in over a year. I cried with joy for the family I'd gained and grief for the families I'd lost. But mostly, I cried with gratitude for the wonderful people fate had allowed into my life.

19

Leaving the grounds of Ridgewick Hall the next day as we travelled to the village for Catherine's wedding felt like walking free of a prison cell. Everyone took a collective sigh of relief as we crossed the property line without officers watching our every move.

The day was warm with a gentle breeze that kept it from feeling too hot. The clear blue sky overhead was the same shade as Catherine's eyes. The perfect weather for her wedding day.

Alice looked lovely in a pale pink lace gown over silk, her brown hair held down with a matching lace band, and she sat next to me in the car ride over to the abbey. Lord and Lady Ashton were in their best—Lord Ashton in a brown suit with a matching bowler hat and Lady Ashton in a dress the same shade of pink as Alice's, though longer and with matching gloves. I wore a neutral green silk gown that hung past my knees in a loose swirl of a hem with black t-strap heels and a black cloche hat, and I felt quite fabulous. Though, no one could compare to Catherine.

Charles Cresswell left for the village abbey early in the morning, before even the sun rose, so he would be surprised by Catherine's gown. And surprised he would be. She was a picture in her dress. It was cut in a V across her neck, delicate beading lining the hem and creating a diamond pattern across the rest of the dress. White gloves covered half of each of her arms, the band ending in a point at her elbow, and she wore a beaded headband with a long lace veil that wrapped around her head and shoulders like a halo. When she came down the stairs in her gown, even Lord Ashton looked a little misty-eyed.

"Can you believe the day is finally here, Catherine?" I asked, leaning into the front seat to pat her shoulder.

She clutched the small bundle of flowers in her hand and grinned at me. "I truly can't. I'm so nervous I think I might shake the beads of my dress loose. Part of me thinks it is all too good to be true, and he'll change his mind at the last moment."

"You have nothing to be nervous about," Alice called. "Charles is insanely in love with you. This day will go off without a hitch. No surprises."

Catherine's lip twitched up at the corner, and she shrugged, turning away from me so I couldn't see her face. "I don't know. There might be a few surprises."

George drove slowly through the town to reach the abbey, and we passed the small cottage where Miss Brown and her sister were living. I wanted to stop and see how she was doing, but there was no time. The ceremony would start in only a few minutes. Besides, I wasn't sure I wanted to see how ill she was. The bumps on my hands had subsided, but I'd woken up that morning with a slightly blue tinge to my fingers and the feeling that my feet weren't settled properly beneath me. Dr. Shaw did his best to counteract the poisons effects, but he told me I would likely still suffer some symptoms. It was a small price to pay for justice.

The Abbey was a large stone building with a pointed arcade out front and two large wooden doors behind it. We crawled out of the car one by one, George offering a hand to help us to our feet, and Lord and Lady Ashton led the way inside.

"Through those doors is your future husband," Alice said, pinching her sister's arm.

Catherine winced and pulled her arm away. "You're going to give me a bruise."

I smiled, amazed that they could find something to argue about even on what was supposed to be the happiest day of Catherine's life. Then, I turned to look down the colonnade, and my smile fell flat.

My heart stuttered to a stop, and my feet must have followed suit because Alice ran into my back and yelped in surprise. Then, she followed my gaze and gasped.

"Is that *him*?"

I didn't answer her. I turned and walked towards him, wondering at what point the hallucination would break, and he would disappear. When I was standing directly in front of him, close enough to reach out and run a hand through his dark hair, I realized he was actually there.

"Achilles," I said softly, almost embarrassed by the obvious sway he held over me.

He wore a dark blue suit with thin stripes that accentuated his lean frame. His dark hair was slicked to one side, and he was holding tightly to the cane he always carried. The one that had a thin blade hidden in the bottom. He looked even more tan than I remembered him, and his dark eyes were shining, crinkled around the corners from his smile.

"Hello, Nellie," he said quietly, his voice warm.

I didn't yet know who I would choose to be moving forward in life, but I liked that I would always be 'Nellie' to Achilles. He was the first person I'd told my secret to, and I liked the idea that he had known the real me all along. He had always known who lurked beneath the surface.

"What are you doing here?" I asked. I looked back over my shoulder, realizing I'd left my family at the doors of the abbey. They were all still standing there, staring at us and clearly eavesdropping on our conversation. When they saw me looking, Lady Ashton quickly pulled open the doors of the church and Alice and Catherine ran inside. I smiled and shook my head.

Achilles took a step towards me and grabbed one of my hands, running his thumb along the knuckles on the back of my hand. "I came here for you, Rose."

My heart leapt at the idea, but I quickly tied it down. "You did not meet me at St. James's Park. I waited for an hour, and—"

"I did not get your message," he said, pulling my hand towards him and pressing it to his chest. "I would have met you. I would have arrived an hour early just to be certain I didn't miss you. Believe me, if I had known you wanted to see me, I would have forgotten all about the case I was working and come back to London immediately. I wanted to be there, but I didn't know."

Part of me—the part that had felt rejected and embarrassed waiting in the park for him—did not want to forgive him so easily, but his excuse made sense. I hadn't knocked on the door or spoken to him. All I'd done was leave a note on his door.

"Do you believe me?" he asked, tilting his head to the side and leaning down to catch my eye.

I nodded. "I suppose I should have ensured you received the message before I assumed you were done with me."

He smiled, his thin mustache twitching up. "Can I talk to you?"

"We are talking," I said, unable to wipe the smile from my lips.

He looked around, glancing behind me. Guests were still streaming through the front doors of the church. I turned to see Aunt Ruth and her girls—all in matching dresses the same shade of brown as the stone walls—walking through the doors. The girls had their heads tipped back, mouths opened as they admired the architecture. Vivian and Charles Barry were behind them. Vivian looked lovely in a violet chiffon gown with long flowing sleeves, a silver hair comb, and black heels. Charles looked nice as he always did in a thick-striped suit, but the frown on his face spoke of a clear distaste for the entire affair. I was slightly worried he would stand up in the middle of the ceremony and declare his love for Catherine, ruining the entire event. Though, in Alice's eyes, his declaration would only add to the excitement of the day.

Every person who passed glanced to where Achilles and I stood off to the side of the main entrance, and I realized our location was not what one could exactly call private.

"Would you like to follow me into the churchyard for a moment?" he asked. "There is something I'd like to discuss with you."

I squeezed his fingers, ready to follow him anywhere, but then I thought of Catherine. "Can I meet you there?"

Achilles narrowed his eyes playfully. "You promise you aren't running away?"

I thought of the morning I'd slipped away from him in Morocco without a goodbye. I would not be so foolish again.

"I promise."

He smiled and nodded, releasing my hand so I could join the guests walking through the front doors and finding seats in the pews. Alice and Lady Ashton were talking off to the side of the church, and I cut across the back of the chapel to reach them.

"Where is Catherine?" I asked.

"She is in the changing room," Alice said. Then, unable to help herself, she whispered, "Is that Achilles Prideaux?"

"Later," I promised with a wink before darting away in the direction of the changing room. I knocked on the solid wooden door and Catherine called for me to come in.

She was standing in front of a long mirror, adjusting

her veil. She turned around as I walked in, and the sight of her almost stole my breath away. "Charles might drop dead when he sees you."

Catherine's eyes went wide. "Let's hope not. There has been more than enough of that lately."

I laughed and then crossed the room. She extended both of her hands to me, pulling me close as though we were dear friends. Which, we were.

"Catherine," I said, looking up at her with a knowing smile, eyebrows raised.

She smiled. "Your heart was broken, Rose. You didn't say so outright, but I could tell. Achilles Prideaux broke your heart, and I thought he deserved a second chance."

"You invited him?" I asked, even though I already knew the answer.

"You were heartbroken," Catherine repeated with emphasis, as if that was reason enough for any action she had decided to take. "I wanted to do whatever I could to ensure you were as happy as I am."

"Did you know he would come?" I asked.

Catherine shook her head. "I simply extended the invitation. Achilles showed up because he wanted to. And because he is smart," she said, nudging me in the hip. "Now, stop talking to me and go talk to him."

"He wants me to meet him in the churchyard," I said, my stomach turning with nerves. "It seemed important."

"Go, go," Catherine urged, grabbing my shoulders and turning me towards the doors. "Skip the wedding if you have to. Just go see what he wants."

"I would never skip your wedding," I assured her.

"But I would not blame you if you did," she said. "He is a very handsome man."

I gasped playfully. "You are soon to be a married woman, Miss Beckingham."

"Soon," she said with a wicked smile. Then, she gave me one final push through the door and closed it behind me before I could argue.

I stood frozen on the other side of the door for a moment. Even just a few days before, my future had been an unknown. I didn't know if I would have the Beckinghams in my life anymore. I didn't know if I would have anyone I could depend upon or anyone who cared about me. And now, just a few days later, I was surrounded by people who accepted and loved me, and I was about to add one more to their number in the form of a very handsome French detective. I had solved a great many mysteries over the previous year, but the greatest of all was my own future. It was a case I would never have been able to crack. The only way to know what would happen was to live it.

So, I took one step and then another, growing more confident with each footfall against the stone floor. Whatever Achilles proposed, I would accept. I had left him behind once, and I had no intention of doing it again.

Want more history and mystery? Try "A Simple Country Murder," Book 1 of the Helen Lightholder Murder Mysteries."

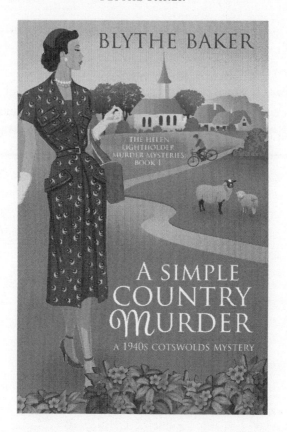

MURDER. Spies. Treason. Shadowy secrets lurk beneath the surface of an idyllic country village...

When Helen Lightholder's world is shattered by the death of her husband during the London Blitz, she escapes to the countryside, hoping to leave the war behind her. But managing an inherited property in a quaint Gloucestershire village turns out to be more perilous than she expects.

Cozy little Brookminster isn't the peaceful haven Helen dreamed of, and it isn't long before she discovers that, even here, dark threats and dangerous secrets await.

As family duty compels her to meddle in a police investigation into the suspicious death of a relative, she finds herself at odds with the local inspector.

Can Helen bring justice to her little corner of the country, while war rages on in the greater world outside? Or will her investigation make her the next target of a fiendish killer who has everything to lose?

ABOUT THE AUTHOR

Blythe Baker is the lead writer behind several popular historical and paranormal mystery serieses. When Blythe isn't buried under clues, suspects, and motives, she's acting as chauffeur to her children and head groomer to her household of beloved pets. She enjoys walking her dog, lounging in her backyard hammock, and fiddling with graphic design. She also likes binge-watching mystery shows on TV.

To learn more about Blythe, visit her website and sign up for her newsletter: www.blythebaker.com